COLD AS ICE

COLD AS ICE

ELIZABETH LEVY

MORROW JUNIOR BOOKS
NEW YORK

Printed in the United States of America.
1   2   3   4   5   6   7   8   9   10

Library of Congress Cataloging-in-Publication Data
Levy, Elizabeth.
Cold as ice / by Elizabeth Levy.
p.   cm.
Summary: Working at the Dome, a sports arena in New York City,
during a pre-Olympic skating exhibition, Kelly meets two competitive
male skaters whose lives become threatened by a string of mysterious
accidents.
ISBN 0-688-06579-1
[1. Ice skating—Fiction.   2. Mystery and detective stories.
3. New York (N.Y.)—Fiction.]   I. Title.
PZ7.L5827Cn 1988

[Fic]—dc19   88-12898
                                                                CIP
                                                                AC

COLD AS ICE

1 Scream Loud!

Chloe and I were late coming home from school. We could hear noises coming from my bedroom, frantic noises of someone or something wanting to get out. The bottom of my door looked like it had been attacked by giant termites. There was a hole in it just big enough for a cold wet nose.

"This is ridiculous," said Chloe. "Hasn't he learned yet that you always come home?"

"Baxter, get back," I yelled as I turned the doorknob and pushed. Baxter was so happy I was home from school that he was jumping against the door.

As soon as I got it open a crack, sixty pounds of ecstatic dog jumped on me. Poor Baxter. He was abandoned once and he never got over it.

I call Baxter a Dome puppy. You've heard of pound puppies, haven't you? Baxter's a Dome puppy. I found him in the Dome.

My mom is head of security for the Empire Dome Sports and Entertainment Complex—at least that's how it's listed in *The New York Times*. But everybody

1

calls it the Dome. After school and on weekends, Chloe and I both work there.

I'm sixteen, a junior at Chelsea High School of Humanities. Chloe Chow is my best friend. She is not only the smartest kid in our class, she has to be one of the prettiest, with long sleek black hair. Sometimes she teases me that I'm her best friend because she's the only girl in our class shorter than I am. But that's not true, and Chloe knows it.

Chloe and I aren't the only ones in our class who have afterschool jobs at the Dome; but because of my mom, we always get the best ones. Tonight and all weekend there was going to be a figure-skating exhibition at the Dome featuring the two male stars from our Olympic team. It wasn't just an exhibition. The skaters would be judged because their coaches wanted to simulate the Olympics. The judges' marks wouldn't "count," except for that one night, but it would still be exciting. Along with the usual hot dogs and popcorn, Chloe and I would be selling roses for fans to throw at the stars. Throwing roses is a skating tradition. I love skating, and I was looking forward to the whole weekend. Some people might think that it's a drag to get out of school Friday and go right to work, but not Chloe and I.

We get to go to rock concerts, basketball games, hockey games, tennis matches—you name it, it's been performed or played at the Dome. We've even seen truck-pulling exhibitions, not to mention the circus and animal shows of every kind. If you love animals, and I do, you'd also love working at the Dome. However, I don't think you'd ever find another Baxter. He's one of a kind. I found him wandering around after a dog show. No one ever claimed him.

Baxter's huge. He looks like a cross between a wolfhound and an Afghan, very elegant-looking. I believe he's a rare breed, perhaps from Sri Lanka or someplace weird like that. Mom thinks that he's a mutt who snuck into the Dome during the dog show, looking for a little action. As she says, we get a lot of characters like that, and a lot of action.

I took Baxter to obedience school. He was very good at playing dead on command. But after a month, Baxter was still peeing on the floor when we left him alone in the house. The trainer said that being alone made Baxter anxious. Mom says that coming home to a house smelling of urine makes her anxious. Baxter feels safe in my bedroom so he stays there when I'm at school, and Mom lets me take him to the Dome when we're both working.

Chloe, Baxter, and I walked from our house to the Dome. The Dome sits on the Hudson River. The neighborhood used to be terrible, a few tenement buildings scattered between empty warehouses and rotting piers. But the Dome has changed all that. Nonetheless, I never mind having Baxter at my side. There are still an awful lot of tough customers around.

I know that some people find it hard to believe, but there are streets in New York that are practically empty, even in the middle of the afternoon. Those are the streets that are the most dangerous. It's not "people" I'm afraid of in New York. It's emptiness, because there's no one to hear you if you scream.

"So who are you going to fall in love with tonight?" Chloe teased. "Will it be Ken Swanson or Andre Emerson? I know you. It'll be one or the other."

"I'm not sure. Ken Swanson is cute, but Andre Emerson is sexy. Maybe Andre. He's rich. My grandmother is always telling me that it's as easy to marry a rich man as a poor one."

"That's so reactionary," said Chloe. "Personally I like Ken Swanson. He's got guts. I think it's romantic that he used to steal cars. I bet you fall in love with Ken Swanson. This time don't stammer when you meet him."

Chloe was teasing me because at almost every event, I get a huge crush on someone. It makes my work that much more interesting. So far, even though I've met a number of my crushes, nothing has happened. But hope springs eternal, and tonight promised to be really interesting.

For the first time in decades, American men's

skating was truly competitive. Andre Emerson had been the skater expected to eventually win a gold medal. Even as a junior, he had been touted as the best American skater in years. He had worked his way from the juniors to the seniors. He scored fifth in the last Olympics, then continued his climb in both the national and international competitions. Then almost out of nowhere, another challenger had appeared.

Ken Swanson came from North Dakota. He had been a hockey star and something of a juvenile delinquent. His wasn't the usual background for a figure skater. According to the newspapers, there was no love lost between the two top contenders. The Olympic coaches had arranged a twelve-city exhibition tour, and the public was loving every minute of it.

I was daydreaming about which of the two skaters would fall in love with me at first sight, and I wasn't paying attention to what was in front of me. The first hint of danger came from Baxter's growl.

I looked up and grabbed Chloe's arm.

Ten feet in front of me, I saw two men struggling. One seemed to be pushing the other, shoving so hard that the person stumbled. I could only see their backs. The two disappeared into an alleyway between two buildings.

"Hey!" I shouted in the loud deep voice that Mom has taught me. She says that the first thing to do when you are in danger is to scream as loudly and as deeply as you can. When needed, I can come out with a foghorn yell.

I let go of Baxter's leash and sprinted up to the alley. Baxter leapt ahead of me, barking all the way.

I reached the alley. A young guy was lying sprawled on a pile of green plastic trash bags. No one else was around.

"Are you okay?" I asked. The guy stood up. He was not much older than I was, dressed in a black-leather bomber jacket and jeans. He had longish silky blond hair, blue eyes, and skin so pale it looked as if he never saw the sun. He looked vaguely familiar, but perhaps that was just from one of my daydreams. He was good-looking.

The earphones of a Walkman were twisted around his neck. He brushed himself off and gave me a smile. "Was that you who screamed? I thought it was a truck driver."

"I saw you being pushed from behind. What happened?" I asked.

"The creep just appeared out of nowhere. He took off at the sound of your voice. He didn't even take my Walkman. Lucky for me you came along."

"Sometimes kids around here get mugged for their leather jackets," said Chloe.

"Well, thanks to you, he didn't get anything."

"We should still get the police," I said. "Did you get a good look at the guy? I never really saw him."

"I didn't see his face," said the boy. "I was sort of tuned out listening to my tape and the next thing I knew, my earphones were around my neck."

"The police precinct's not far. We'll take you," I offered.

"I don't have time for the police," the boy said.

"But . . . but, you really should," I said.

The guy wasn't paying any attention to me. He knelt down and scratched Baxter under his chin. "You're the ones who really saved my life," he said. Baxter's tail was going a mile a minute.

"Look, I really do have to be going," he said as he stood up. "Thanks again." He walked away quickly.

Chloe stared after him. "That was scary, but he was one cute guy," she said. "You should have gotten his name. It would have been so romantic, you saving his life. And somehow, I thought I knew him."

"He was more interested in Baxter than me, but you're right. He sure was cute. Still, he was awfully casual about being attacked. It was weird."

"Yeah, well this isn't the safest block in New York," said Chloe. "Let's get out of here."

We hurried to work. Just another typical afternoon in my hometown, the Big Apple.

2 To Die For

At the Dome's employees' entrance, Chloe and I waved our identification cards and pushed through the revolving door. My ID to the Dome is worth its weight in gold. You can't imagine what I've been offered for it by kids at school who want to get close to their favorite rock stars.

The guard, Stuart, took out a metal detector and scanned it up and down my jeans and my sweat shirt, and then did Chloe. He even ran it across Baxter, as if maybe he had a bomb hidden in his mouth. Then he motioned us through.

"What's going on?" I asked Stuart. "A bomb threat?" The Dome does get more than its share of bomb threats.

"I just got orders that they want heavy security for tonight," said Stuart. "I wouldn't think skaters would be such a big deal."

"It's probably because it's pre-Olympics," I said. "I'll find out what's going on when I drop Baxter off."

Chloe went on to the locker room, and I took Baxter up the staff elevator to Mom's office. I was anxious to tell Mom about how Baxter and I had saved that boy on the street. It certainly was strange. I think I was more shook up by it than the guy who got mugged.

Judy, Mom's assistant, sat in the outer office. She greeted Baxter with a Milk-Bone from the supply she keeps in her desk. The door to Mom's office was closed.

"Is she there?" I asked Judy.

"She's with Mr. Dellinger," answered Judy. "Remember, he's a skating freak, and he wants security tight. Especially since we're so close to the Olympics."

"That explains why Baxter had to go through the metal detector," I said.

Watson Dellinger III is the director of the Dome. He comes from a wealthy family and doesn't have to work for a living, but he loves being a big shot in New York. He built the Dome with some of his own money, and he is part owner of both the basketball and hockey teams. He likes to see himself in the newspaper posed with sports stars. A picture of Watson with an Olympic skater hangs right above Judy's desk. The skater has a slightly nervous look, which seems natural since Watson is pulling on the ribbon of the medal that's around her neck.

The door to Mom's office opened, and Mom escorted Watson out. She was more dressed up than usual in a wheat-colored wool suit with a silk shirt the same color. Her hair is blond with streaks of gray in it.

Watson's hair is pure white and he has a perpetual tan, in spite of all the warnings about too much sun causing skin cancer. He looks terrific. He treated me to one of his megawatt smiles.

"Hello there, Kristin," he said. "Baxter, you're looking particularly peppy today."

"It's Kelly, sir," I said politely, trying not to make too much of the fact that he could remember my dog's name but not mine.

Mom winked at me. She says that Watson isn't a bad boss; you just have to treat him with the respect he thinks he deserves. Watson would like it if I greeted him with a curtsy, and then backed out of the room. I don't do that for anybody, even my mom's boss, but I do try to call him *sir*.

Watson turned back to my mother. "So you're confident that you've done all that's necessary."

"Watson, we've protected the President of the United States and other heads of state with less fuss."

I realized that this was not a great time to tell Mom and Watson I had interrupted a mugging only two blocks from the Dome.

Mom continued with her list of precautions. "As I told you before, Watson, I've called in extra security. We'll treat it like a rap concert. Everyone will go through a metal detector."

Her voice was superpolite, but underneath she gave the clear impression that Watson had better leave her alone to do her job. Before she took this job at the Dome, Mom had been a police officer with the New York Police Department for fifteen years, specializing in security and crowd control. Dellinger might be used to being the boss, but let me tell you, so is my mom. Mom will never be Watson's flunky, and he knows it.

Watson had just reached the door leading from Mom's outer office to the corridor of the executive suites when the door swung inward, almost throwing him off his feet.

Two men burst into the room, and one of them was the guy who had been attacked on the street! We stared at each other.

"Did you follow me?" he demanded.

My mouth dropped open—of all the arrogance! Then I noticed a black snakeskin skate bag. That's when I recognized him. He was Ken Swanson. No wonder he had looked familiar.

He looked at me and laughed, as if I had played an incredible joke on him. I giggled, too, but it was a nervous cackle.

The other man was tall with graying hair and a mustache that curled up at each end, like the villain in a cartoon. He didn't even notice that Ken and I had recognized each other. He was shouting at Watson. "We're in trouble. I worried about coming to New York. You promised in New York we'd be safe. Ha! My skater has been threatened. Something must be done."

Watson looked at my mother as if to say, "I told you so."

"Serge, this is Ann Ross. She is my head of security. Ann, this is Serge Cohasset, the renowned Olympic coach, and Ken Swanson." Watson raised his voice. "Hello, Ken."

Ken was still shaking his head at me. "I don't believe it's you," he said. "Are you sure you didn't follow me here?"

"No," I protested. "I work here. I didn't know who you were when I saw you on the street. Without skates, it's hard to recognize you."

"Thanks, that's good for my ego."

"Kelly, what's going on?" asked Mom. "Have you two met before?"

"I just saw Ken get mugged on the street a few minutes ago," I said.

"You got mugged and you didn't tell me about it?" screeched his coach. Serge Cohasset had been born in Sweden, and although he had lived here for many years and was a United States citizen, he had an accent like the crazy Swedish chef from the Muppets.

"I didn't want to make a big deal out of it," said

Ken. "Nothing really happened. This kid here saved me."

I wasn't sure that I liked being called "this kid."

Baxter's tail had been wagging like a metronome ever since Ken entered the room. He bent down to pat him.

"We have no time for dogs," said Serge angrily.

"This dog helped save my life," said Ken. He smiled at me. He was giving Baxter a rubdown right behind his ears, the exact place that causes Baxter to fall in love. I wondered how Ken had found Baxter's favorite spot so quickly.

"Show them the note," said Serge Cohasset. He waved his hands dramatically at Mom and Watson. "Not only was Ken attacked; he got a death threat! You must agree with me. With all that's been happening, Ken must not perform!"

Ken stopped patting Baxter and stared Serge down. It was an arrogant look. "I'll perform against Andre," said Ken. "I'll be out there tonight and I'll beat the pants off him. So don't . . ." Ken paused. Whatever he was going to say, it was not going to be polite.

Mom stepped in to take back control of her office. "I'd like to see this death threat," she said.

"It was found in his dressing room," said Serge.

"Let me see it," said my mother in her best officer's voice.

Ken's jeans were so tight that he had to struggle

to get a piece of lined yellow paper out of his back pocket. It was a struggle I didn't mind watching.

He handed the paper to my mother. "Ken, you are to die for," Mom read.

I giggled. Ken looked at me and winked.

"Why is that young lady laughing?" Serge demanded.

"I'm sorry," I said. "It's just that 'to die for' is an American expression. It means that the person has a crush on him."

"Crush?" asked Serge.

"Thinks he's cute," I said. I could feel my cheeks turn red.

Serge took the letter from my mother. " 'To die for'? This is something young girls say?" He was staring at me.

I nodded. "Well, not all young girls, but a lot of them."

"Where did you find this note?" Mom asked Ken.

"It was in my dressing room with some flowers," said Ken. "It was unsigned. I told Serge it was nothing to worry about."

"You told me not to worry. You didn't tell me it was an American expression. It's not the same thing. And now you've been attacked."

Serge was right. There's a world of difference between telling someone not to worry and explaining. I should know. Mom does both. It's when she tells me not to worry that I get scared. When she

14

explains, I calm down. To her credit, Mom explains most of the time.

Serge looked at my mother and Watson. "So you think I overreacted?"

Mom shook her head. "No, not at all. I'd like to know the details of this mugging."

Ken shrugged. "I thought muggings were standard in New York. It all happened so quickly, I never saw the guy's face. He grabbed me from behind and shoved."

"I saw that," I added.

"What were you doing outside of the Dome?" demanded Serge. "You should have known it wasn't safe."

"I'm not on your leash," said Ken. His voice was soft, and he kept his hand petting Baxter. "I needed a break. It wasn't my time to practice. The girls were on the ice. Relax. It wasn't even a successful mugging. He didn't take anything."

"I do wish you had gone to the police right away or come to me," said Mom.

"I told you I hardly saw the guy," said Ken. "He ran away when he saw Baxter here."

"But what if the mugging and that death threat are connected?" asked Serge.

"That seems farfetched," said my mother. "Unfortunately muggings around the Dome aren't unusual. But I'd like Ken to leave that note with me. I think you were right to bring it to my attention.

I'd like you to report to me any other incidents, no matter how 'silly' they seem. We already have extra security on for tonight because Watson seemed to feel that the skating community could be under some kind of threat."

"Before the Olympics, you can't be too careful," said Watson.

"I would like to see this extra security," said Serge.

"I'll be glad to show it to you," said Mom, "as well as our SOP."

"SOP?" asked Serge.

Mom smiled. "Excuse me. Every job has its own shorthand. I never could figure out all those skating terms. SOP just stands for our Standard Operating Procedure. We've had many events for which we beef up security. For example, tonight all ticket holders go through metal detectors. I'm about to go on my rounds checking with the staff. Would you like to accompany me?"

"I would be most interested," said Serge.

"I wouldn't," said Ken. "I'd like to get back to the dressing room. Serge, it's almost time for my final run-through."

"I will meet you by the ice," said Serge. "Andre is practicing now."

"Is there a way I can get back without going through the main lobby?" asked Ken. "On our way up, I noticed some kids had already arrived."

"I'd rather not have you wandering around by yourself," said Mom.

"I'll take him," I said. "I have to get dressed, too."

"Get dressed? Are you one of the local skaters who are promenading with us?" Ken asked.

"Uh, no. I can't really skate. But we have to wear special uniforms at the concessions. Wait till you see the little domed hats."

Mom coughed and glanced at Watson. I had forgotten that he had designed our uniforms himself.

"Kelly almost was a skater," said Mom to cover up for my gaffe.

I groaned. I knew there was no way to stop her from telling my skating story. It was so embarrassing. I mean, if you just met a gorgeous boy, would you want your mom to tell him a story about sucking your thumb?

"When Kelly was about five, I took her skating in Central Park," said my mother. "She put on her skates, went out on the ice, fell down, picked herself up, and said to me, 'Now that I'm a skater, I no longer suck my thumb.'"

Ken looked at me. He could see I was dying of embarrassment, but he teased me anyhow.

"And did you do it?" he asked.

"Do what?"

"Stop sucking your thumb?" he asked.

17

"She never sucked her thumb again," said my mother.

Ken smiled at me. "So you're a skater."

I shook my head. "I liked going fast, but I could never learn to go backward. What can I tell you? I don't have eyes in the back of my head."

Serge interrupted. "Enough of this. I want you to practice the new routine before your performance. I'll meet you at the rink after I inspect the security."

Ken nodded, but he kept his blue eyes on me. Then he grinned at me. He did have a wonderful smile.

I tell you this guy really was to die for.

3 A Backstage Tour

The public side of the Dome deserves its reputation as one of the seven wonders of the modern world. The central arena's light fixture has been photographed so many times that it is instantly recognizable. It was designed by a famous sculptor to reflect the intensity of New York. She certainly got that right; at its full strength, it's dazzling. It looks a bit like the Statue of Liberty's crown.

However, the underside of the Dome is definitely not luxury or high-tech. Because the arena itself is elliptical, the corridors all curve and they all look the same—just blank winding cement walls with no posters or pretty painted stripes like in the public areas, not even pictures of Watson Dellinger III. The problem with the back corridors is that you're never exactly sure where you are. It's extremely easy to get lost if you don't know your way around the place.

"Are you sure you're not just taking me in circles?" Ken asked.

"Trust me," I said. "I'll have you there in a minute."

Ken laughed and repeated, " 'Trust me.' People say that all the time. How many times do you think they mean it?"

"I was just making a joke," I said. "But you can trust me. At least in getting around the Dome. The Dome and I grew up together. They broke ground for it the year I was born. My mom and I live just a few blocks away."

Ken smiled. "Relax, Kelly. I'm just teasing. What about your dad?"

"He and Mom are divorced. You tease a lot, don't you?"

"Can't you take it?" he asked.

"I can take it," I answered.

I glanced back at him. We were curving around the corridor that led to the main concession area. We practically collided with Chloe and Jesse, who were holding hands. There was nothing unusual about that. Chloe and Jesse Hernandez have been inseparable for three months now. Jesse's a senior at Chelsea Humanities, and Chloe and I got him a job at the Dome.

"Chloe, Jesse, meet Ken Swanson," I said, rather proudly. It's not often that I get to shock Chloe.

"You're Ken Swanson! No wonder I thought I knew you," shrieked Chloe. "The last time I saw you, you were lying on a pile of garbage bags."

Ken laughed. "You know, New York is smaller than my hometown. You keep running into the same people. I never expected to see either of you again. Are you here for the show?"

"We're here to make money off you," said Chloe. "We plan on selling enough roses to fill the rink."

"But won't you be throwing any?" Ken asked.

"They cost too much," said Jesse, stepping forward.

"Ken, this is Jesse Hernandez," said Chloe. "He gets all my roses."

Chloe was so cool. She stood between Ken and Jesse, flirting with them both. Now if it was me, I would be stammering and doing the curly shuffle. Chloe has had a string of boyfriends. I'm at the stage in which every guy turns out to be just a friend for life. I'm hoping it won't be permanent. I might as well tell you now that except for kissing games, I have never had a real soul kiss. And I bet you thought New York teenagers were fast.

"I can't believe you found him again," Chloe whispered. "It's so romantic."

"Just don't tell him he's to die for," I mumbled back.

"Well, he is," Chloe said.

"What are you two whispering about?" Ken asked.

"You," said Chloe.

"I thought so," said Ken. Chloe and I exchanged looks. Was there no end to this guy's ego?

21

"Come on," I said to Ken. "I'm supposed to get you back to your dressing room. Your coach wanted you on the ice."

"Want to come with us, Chloe?" Ken asked.

Jesse grabbed Chloe's hand, and I had a feeling that her knuckles would be red when he let go.

Ken must have noticed Jesse's expression. It was hard not to. Jesse looked like he wanted to flatten Ken.

"Hey, I was only kidding," Ken said to Jesse. "I know she's taken. You're just a lucky guy."

"Taken," Chloe teased. "What do you think I am, a piece of clothing? 'Sorry, that dress is taken.' Where did you grow up, in a box?"

Ken burst out laughing. "I thought everyone knew." He lowered his voice. "I grew up on a small struggling family farm in North Dakota. I was a poor boy who never learned any manners."

"I hear that Andre Emerson is teaching you a little humility," said Jesse. "You don't exactly have a clear path to the gold."

Ken's teasing manner changed. "I'd say it's the other way around," he said. "I'm the one who's going to take it away from Andre."

"I saw you on television in Boston," said Jesse smoothly. "Your fall when you tried for the quad looked bad. I was surprised you weren't hurt."

I saw that fall, too. Ken had tried to do four

revolutions in the air—the quadruple jump. It had taken him several seconds to stand up, and the rest of his routine had been very shaky.

Ken took my hand as casually as if we had known each other for years. "Come on, Kelly. If I don't get in a practice session, Andre really won't have anything to worry about tonight. Maybe you'll bring me luck."

Just then the entire corridor filled with the smell of boiled hot dogs and Ben-Gay. It was a smell that could only come from one guy—Marc Stone, who just started working at the Dome this fall. Marc wears a neatly trimmed beard that I think is supposed to make him look older. He's very cute, in a cuddly bear sort of way, but he'd look cuter without the beard.

Marc is on the maintenance crew and some nights he also staffs the concessions. Too bad he always smells of Ben-Gay. I've told him he would probably sell more hot dogs if he'd lay off the weight lifting. I tease him about his real work being his body. He's got great biceps. He was carrying the aluminum hotbox for the hot dogs—which I can hardly lift—as if it weighed nothing.

Chloe is convinced that Marc has a crush on me. I'm not sure. He's never asked me out. I wouldn't mind, Ben-Gay and all. He's just eighteen, and I know he's ambitious. He's told me that on nights he doesn't work at the Dome, he takes classes. I don't know where he finds the time.

"Hi, Kelly," he said. He nodded at Chloe and Jesse. I smiled. I was glad he said hello to me first. Most guys would have chosen Chloe.

I introduced Marc to Ken. "I've heard a lot about you," said Marc. "An amazing rise and all that . . ."

"Yeah, well, nobody remembers that I've been skating since I was two," said Ken. "And while they don't like to put it in the publicity mill, my mom was a figure skater, and before I played hockey, she used to teach me figures."

"So it's not the most amazing story ever told?" asked Jesse. "The punk hockey skater turned graceful swan."

Ken laughed. "Everybody loves 'the hockey player saved by Serge' story. So does Serge."

"Serge Cohasset?" asked Marc. "I've read a lot about him. Is he with you tonight?"

"When is he not with me? That's the question."

"I met him up in Mom's office," I said. "He's something else. His mustache is even funnier-looking in real life than it is on television."

"I'd like to meet him," said Marc. "He's coached a lot of champions. He's supposed to be tough."

"Come to my dressing room after the show," said Ken. "Believe me, Serge will be there, telling me what I did wrong."

"Are you going to be there, Kelly?" Marc asked.

Marc's voice had an intensity to it that was flattering. Maybe Chloe was right. Maybe he did like me.

"I don't know if I'm invited," I said.

"I'd like you all to come by after the show. I need a little moral support on this tour. It hasn't been all roses." Ken's voice had changed. I had a feeling that while the media might be having a heyday with the hot competition on this tour, it wasn't easy to live through.

"Sure, I'll be there," I said. "I can't wait till tonight's performance."

"Neither can the rest of us," said Marc. "I'll come. If I don't get lost again wandering around this place. Dressing rooms are probably labeled Z."

"What are you talking about?" asked Ken.

"Haven't you noticed? There are almost no signs here in the back of the Dome. All the doors are labeled with letters," I said.

"It's to confuse us," said Marc.

"That's not true," I argued. "Although I've got to admit that all new employees complain about the labeling system."

"Good," said Marc. "I'm glad I'm not the only one who feels like a dummy."

The labeling system was Watson Dellinger's idea, not Mom's. Watson is something of a security nut.

Mom says that some of his ideas are good, but he's not a professional. Anyhow, for security reasons the doors to the various service areas are all labeled with letters instead of the names of the services—maintenance is *G*, concessions is *D*, the lighting booth is *A*. The theory is that if we were under any kind of siege, it would make it harder for the terrorists to find their way around.

In the decade since the Dome was opened, most of our security problems have been pickpockets, scalpers, and the fistfights at hockey games. Mom has a reputation for running a very tight ship. We have had only four deaths: three heart attacks and one stabbing. Mom's guards caught the stabber in minutes.

We've had bomb threats, but as far as I know, the elaborate labeling system has confused only the newcomers on the staff, not terrorists. Mom would like to junk the system. She argues that we have such a turnover in employees and give so many backstage tours that the system is useless. But Watson likes it because he invented it.

"How do you know where we are," Ken asked, "if none of the labels make sense?"

"Luckily, I've got a good memory. See this door," I said, pointing to a metal door with the letter *A* on it. "All the lighting controls are here. It's all done by computer."

"Can I see?"

"Sure." The lighting controls are on our standard backstage tour. Everyone wants to see how we change the light bulbs on the crown. It looks very mysterious but actually it's the same system that's been used in theaters for centuries. The crown is suspended on cables that can be lowered to ground level when a bulb needs to be changed.

We all went crowding into the lighting booth. Hal, the head of our lighting crew, waved to me. He was used to me taking VIPs through before a show. Ken walked over to the balcony. At this point, the famous lighting fixture was at eye level, and it looked gigantic. Actually it's much less beautiful close up than it is when you look up at it from the arena.

"Impressed?" I asked.

"Yes," said Ken. "Very. And with you. You seem to know everybody who works in this place, and everybody knows you."

"I don't know everybody, but I bet Mom does. Of course, she's got to vet all employment records before someone gets hired, but she likes to meet the new employees in person, even us kids who sell hot dogs."

"I'd better stick with skating. With my record, I'd never get a job here," said Ken.

"Mom believes in giving people a second chance," I said.

"Well, I'd need thirteen chances."

"You're getting them, aren't you? Isn't that what this tour is all about?" Chloe asked.

"It's about raising money for the Olympic fund," said Ken. "But some people say it's unfair to Andre. It's giving me a chance to go head to head against him. We get judged every night, but the marks don't count for anything. It's getting me used to the competition."

"Serge's the one who gave you your big chance, isn't he?" Marc asked.

"Serge and others," said Ken. "Come on, please don't make me list all the people I'm supposed to thank. I have to do that too often."

"Sorry," said Marc.

Ken put a hand on my arm. "Thanks for taking me on the tour. I've seen all I need. Let's go. I'm always on edge before a performance, and tonight there's a lot riding on it."

"I thought it was just an exhibition," said Marc.

Ken laughed. "And I'm exhibit A. Forget it. I'm just too tightly wound today. You'd better get me on the ice. It's time for my final practice. Want to watch?"

"I'll be there in a minute," said Marc. "I've got something to do here."

"We can't watch now," said Jesse. "We've only got an hour before work, and we need to eat before we sell other people hot dogs." Chloe winked at me when Jesse said "we." But she didn't object. Besides, I think she wanted to give me a chance to be alone with Ken. It's great to have such a loyal best friend. If only I could hire Chloe to flirt for me. But actually, Ken was such a good flirt himself that all I had to do was follow his lead.

4 A Polite Warning

I discovered a new rule. All skaters tower above mere mortals. When I was standing next to Ken at rinkside during the final run-through—he in his skates and skateguards, me in my purple sneakers—I felt I'd shrunk about a foot. And Ken wasn't that tall. Maybe I'd have to take up skating again. It certainly adds inches to your height.

Ken kept glancing at Serge. Serge was in deep conversation with a black skater whom I recognized as Andre Emerson.

Andre had been practicing his routine. He had stopped in the middle, even though to me it hadn't looked as if he had made a mistake. Maybe he was just exhausted. He could hardly breathe. He held his hands along his back over his kidneys, as if somebody had just punched him. His long legs and reed-slim torso were probably steel inside, but they gave him a fragile look compared to Ken's shorter and more compact body.

A blond woman in a silver-fox fur hovered behind Serge and Andre. They both listened to Serge as if he was a guru dispensing the wisdom of the ages, but Serge's attention was completely on Andre. He made soothing noises as if he was talking to a skittish colt. Then Andre pushed away from the side and floated onto the ice to finish his routine, doing impossible turns and making it look easy.

Andre's great skill was how simple he made it all look. He never seemed to hurry. He gathered speed as he skated backward, and then he jumped in the air, his body a tight spiral. He landed with one foot extended.

Ken grunted as if he had been the one making the effort. Serge applauded. I did, too, until I caught the look Ken gave me.

Andre skated back over to Serge and discussed the jump he had made. Serge said something to the woman standing next to him, with a gesture that made me think he didn't want her eavesdropping. She turned and climbed the stairs into the stands, taking each step with a giant stride. Her head was down and she bumped into Marc, who was coming down to meet us.

I thought I saw the woman look over at me and point. I wondered who she was and why she was so interested in me.

She stopped her ascent into the stands, turned away from Marc, and came back down to Ken and me. Marc had disappeared.

31

"Who are you?" the woman asked me before she had even reached us. It was not a polite question.

"Her name's Kelly Ross," said Ken. "I invited her to the practice. Kelly, meet Mrs. Clifton."

"It's supposed to be a closed practice," said the woman.

"Kelly works here," said Ken.

I was beginning to feel as if I only existed in the third person. "How do you do?" I said, sticking out my hand.

The woman lowered her eyes and looked down her nose at me. It made her a little cross-eyed. She ignored my outstretched hand and spoke to Ken.

"I heard that you were attacked outside the Dome. Why was I the last to find out?" She made it sound as if her not knowing about it was worse than Ken's being mugged.

"I'm sorry, Mrs. Clifton," said Ken. "Next time I'm mugged, I'll be sure you're the first to know."

"Ken," warned Mrs. Clifton. "You know there's a limit to my patience."

To my surprise, Ken was immediately contrite. "I'm sorry, Mrs. Clifton, I should have let you know. It just happened a little while ago."

Mrs. Clifton shook her head. "I cannot tolerate secrets," she said.

Then she stood up, went back to Serge, and whispered something in his ear, glancing at me. She made me feel like a speck of dirt.

Ken winked at me. "Sorry about that. She doesn't like strangers around me."

"Who is she?"

"You haven't heard of Carey Clifton? I forget she's only famous in our world. Your Watson Dellinger knows her. Like him, she adopts ice skaters. Right now, I'm her project."

"Adopt? You don't mean literally?" I remembered reading somewhere that Ken was raised by his grandfather.

Ken shook his head. "No, she doesn't have to do that. She usually buys a skater every year, but until me, she's never had a winner. I shouldn't be so cynical. I would never be here without her. She pays for my training. I guess she probably does own me. She puts about eighty-five thousand a year into the 'skating fund' that's earmarked for my expenses. She pays Serge, my travel expenses, even my food."

"Eighty-five thousand? That's a fortune!"

"Well, think of the money she's lost on the losers she backed before me," said Ken.

"What does she get if you win?" I asked.

"The glory," said Ken. "But lately I think she's worried that I might not bring her the right kind of glory. She thinks I should perfect my dancing skills and forget about nailing the quad. Her money doesn't buy her the right to tell me what to do artistically. She even tries to tell Serge what to do with me. It's getting to be a real mess." Ken paused. "I shouldn't be telling you all this."

"It's okay. I'm outside your world. Sometimes it helps just to blurt things out."

"I bet people are always blurting things out to you, Kelly," said Ken. I hadn't realized it, but what Ken said was true. It made me feel good about myself, and good about Ken that he noticed. This wasn't just flirting. It was making a friend.

Just then Serge walked over to us. "You're late," he said.

"We ran into some of the kids Kelly knows in the corridors," said Ken. "I got talking. And Kelly gave me a mini backstage tour. I thought you'd spend more time with Ms. Ross going over the security."

"The security in this complex is the best," said Serge. "It's you I was worried about. Get out there."

Ken took off his skateguards and handed them to me, as if having a lackey was perfectly normal. He shook his legs like a swimmer about to plunge into the water, and then he was gone.

When I've watched skaters on television, what awes me is the blend of music and motion. But when I watched Ken skate without music, boy, was he noisy! His steel blades sounded as if they were cutting through steel, not across ice.

He whipped by at a speed much faster than New York traffic moves on one of our better days. I couldn't take my eyes off him. Though his legs moved slowly, he went fast, like a bicycle in high gear. His skating was so different from Andre's. It was hard to imagine Andre falling. Ken looked as if each jump might be his last. Almost all his jumps started with him facing away from the jump and then landing backward.

Ken missed his very first jump, and then his second.

"His timing's off again," said a voice behind me. "Mrs. C's right. He should forget about the quad and just skate." I turned to see Andre Emerson wiping the sweat off his face.

"You looked great out there," I said.

Andre nodded as if he expected the compliment. "You a friend of Ken's?"

"I just met him. I'm Kelly Ross. I work here. My mom's head of security."

"Aren't you a little bit young to be a security guard?"

"That's not my job. I sell hot dogs and roses."

Andre smiled. "Who do you think will get more roses tonight, Ken or I?" He pointed his thumb at Ken.

"You both deserve them," I said.

"Yeah," said Andre. "But there can only be one winner." He picked up his towel and stared out onto the ice, studying Ken's moves.

"Is it tough having the same coach?" I asked.

"Serge's the best," said Andre. "He always coaches winners. A lot of coaches take on skaters who compete against each other. Serge doesn't have to choose between Ken and me. As he says, that's the judges' job. Besides, I like having Ken where I can keep an eye on him."

I wasn't sure whether Andre was kidding or not. He went over to Serge and whispered something. It seemed as if everybody liked to whisper in Serge's ear. Then Andre came back. "Hope you sell a lot of roses," he said as he picked up his equipment bag.

"Good luck," I said.

"The same to you," said Andre, and I wasn't sure whether he was referring to Ken or my sale of roses. Then he disappeared down the runway toward the dressing area.

Ken skated over to Serge. I could hear Serge crooning to Ken in the same tone that he had used with Andre.

Ken shook his head. "It was crooked in the air," I heard Ken say.

It? I wondered. Ken talked about the quadruple jump as if it still sat out there. Ken went back out onto the ice and Serge followed him in his street shoes. They stood over the patch of ice where the jump had given Ken trouble. They kept looking down as if the ice had been the problem, not the difficulty of the jump. Serge gestured with his hands, making tight movements of one fist over the other. Then Serge came back to rinkside and Ken tried the jump again. This time he almost landed it perfectly, but at the last moment the edge of his skate blade dug into the ice, and he fell down hard.

Ken picked himself up just as the Zamboni machine came out onto the far end of the ice. The loud motor of the Zamboni made it impossible to hear what Serge was shouting to Ken. The Zamboni machine looks as if it belongs out on the street cleaning up garbage. It gobbles up the chips of ice that the skaters make with their blades. Then it lays down new water, leaving a surface smooth as glass.

Wherever I've skated, the rink is always cleared for the Zamboni. But Ken barely seemed to notice it was there. He skated out of the way as the machine came near him, not even giving the operator a glance. I was so engrossed in watching that I didn't notice that Mrs. Clifton had sat down beside me.

She tapped me on the shoulder. "It's so important that Ken not be distracted during this final push to the Olympics," she said.

I guess I was the distraction. I didn't have an answer for her, so I just nodded politely.

"Skaters are peculiar," she continued. "They must be on their own at such a young age that they learn to fake being a good friend. They look as if they're rock steady, but underneath, they're very fragile, even unstable."

This lady was something else. I hadn't known Ken for a half hour and she was warning me off. "Ken doesn't seem unstable," I said, trying not to bite the words off. I had to remember that I had been brought up always to be polite to adults.

"Well, you know he spent time in prison."

"That's a bit of an exaggeration," I said. "As I read it, it was a juvenile correction home. That's quite a difference. My mom was a cop."

"How interesting," said Mrs. Clifton. "And your father?"

"He's a cop, too. But Mom and he are divorced."

Mrs. Clifton looked at me as if I were an exotic species, the offspring of two police officers.

"Then you should be used to people who are not as stable as they seem," said Mrs. Clifton. "I'm afraid Ken picked up some bad tendencies in prison . . ." She corrected herself and gave me a cool smile. ". . . in the juvenile correction facility."

"I just met Ken," I said. "But there doesn't seem to be anything crazy about him."

"Now, my dear, I was just warning you," said Mrs. Clifton. "You know, I always speak my mind. It sometimes bothers people, but I believe in telling the truth."

I bet she believed in stepping on ants, too. I hate

it when people take pride in saying stuff that hurts and then gloat about being honest.

Mrs. Clifton looked down her nose at me again. "I think," she said, "an investment in people is the best investment you can make. However, like the stock market, you can't always expect a winner."

"Yes, ma'am," I said. I was glad that I was nobody's investment, particularly hers. I wouldn't want to owe Mrs. Clifton the time of day.

Ken skated over to us, then stopped short, sending slivers of ice flying in front of him. His face was flushed. He looked happy. "Did you see that, Mrs. C? I almost landed it."

Mrs. Clifton smiled at him. "Almost, Ken? Is almost good enough?"

Ken's face deflated. "I thought you were terrific," I said.

"Almost," muttered Ken. Then he looked defiant. He had one of the most changeable faces I had ever seen. "Mrs. C, you're right. Almost isn't good enough."

Mrs. Clifton smiled at him, then nodded to me as if to tell me that she had won that round. And I hadn't even known we were in a fight.

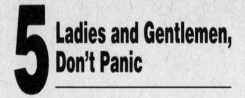

5 Ladies and Gentlemen, Don't Panic

Chloe and I were able to watch the exhibition on one of the closed-circuit television sets that were placed at every concession stand. The TVs weren't for us. They were for the paying customers, so that people could buy souvenirs and food without missing any action.

However, as the performance of the local skaters drew to an end, we decided that we wanted to watch Andre and Ken closer up. I wasn't going to watch Ken on TV when I could see him live. Besides, we only had about a half-dozen roses left. I figured maybe I could throw a few myself.

We got Jesse to take over our stand, then ducked down the back staircase so we could watch at rinkside. After all, there are some perks to being the head of security's daughter.

We came out near the performers' entrance. Serge nodded to me. His arms were folded across his chest. The judges were to our left, but they looked less judgmental than Serge.

I caught a glimpse of Ken as he skated out to the center of the rink. He was like a prince presenting himself. Now, instead of jeans and a T-shirt, he was dressed in a skintight blue jumpsuit with a dramatic silver *V* across his chest.

A wild sound went up from the crowd. I've been at lots of rock concerts, but this sound was higher-pitched—maybe because so many young girls love skating.

Ken skated to a score with such a powerful back-beat that the audience was almost forced to clap along. Ken was the Tina Turner of skaters. He might not be as elegant a skater as Andre, but he made you feel good watching him. He grinned at the audience, almost inviting us to come out there and try it with him.

Ken skated as if the music were the walls and he could climb them. He played to his audience. There was nothing interior about Ken's skating. His blue eyes flashed out to the audience, bringing us into the spins with him. No wonder he hated Mrs. Clifton telling him to be more artistic. Ken had a style all his own.

He was landing his double and triple jumps on the money. When he came out of one triple jump, landing on one edge, he raised a fist in the air, punching out the beat.

The audience loved him. "Now I know why we sold so many roses," whispered Chloe. "He's terrific."

"I know," I said. "As soon as he's done, I'm going to throw my roses at him, too."

Ken was doing a flying camel with his back almost parallel to the ice, his arms spread wide as if he were a young god presenting himself for sacrifice. It was a move more familiar to female skaters because men are rarely so flexible. He kept bending farther and farther backward until he was almost in a backbend.

Then he lifted himself. It was as if his upper body were made of helium balloons. He skated faster and faster around the perimeter of the rink. As he sped past where we were standing, I was sure that his eyes had flashed on Chloe and me. I bet you that every girl in the Dome felt the same way, as if he was skating just for her. Then he lifted himself into the air, trying for the quadruple jump. He came out way too fast, only completing a double, but the expression on his face didn't change, even though the crowd groaned its disappointment.

He raised his arms around his head to go into his final spin, then spun so fast that his skintight costume was a blur.

The crowd went wild. He stopped, a huge grin on his face. He opened his arms out wide, drinking in our applause. No wonder Andre was worried. Ken might not be as good technically, but he was just so exciting to watch.

Then Ken skated over to our end. Serge put his

arm around him. "Surprised you with that back-bend, huh?" gasped out Ken.

Serge laughed. "Yes . . . it made up for missing the quad."

Ken's eyes scanned the judges' table as they scribbled in their notebooks.

I held my roses, waiting for an appropriate moment to give them to him.

Andre took off his skateguards and handed them to Serge without saying a word to Ken. Andre was to be the final performer of the night. I didn't envy him having to skate after Ken.

Andre went out onto the far end of the ice and nervously skated in circles, waiting for the judges to put up their scores for Ken.

The applause for Ken was so great that Serge pushed him back out onto the ice to take a curtain call.

Along the sides of the rink, dozens of flowers were being thrown in Ken's direction. He skated to pick them up, pausing to kiss the cheek of one little girl in a ponytail.

"Give him yours when he skates by," Chloe whispered.

The judges' bell rang, indicating they were ready to give their scores.

Ken skated back our way. I threw my roses as high as I could so that they would fall at Ken's feet.

My eyes followed my throw—that's how I happened to be looking up when it happened. If I believed in ESP, I'd say that the building spoke to me, telling me that something was wrong.

Andre was at the far end of the rink, completing his warm-ups, and Ken was skating toward me, his arms full of roses. I was looking straight up when one of the cables holding the light fixture snapped. I watched as the point fell, straight from the crown down onto the ice. It landed on its tip, vibrating back and forth.

It landed closer to Andre than to Ken, about where the hockey blue line showed faintly through the ice. Ken slammed into the railing next to us.

Chloe tells me that I screamed, but I don't remember, and I'm sure no one except Chloe could hear me above the roar of the crowd.

Ken's eyes were bulging. I looked up and could see the naked floodlights behind the fractured crown.

At the far end of the ice, Andre stood stiff-legged, his mouth a round O. He seemed in shock, and he kept staring up at the ceiling as if he expected the rest of the light fixture to fall on him.

Suddenly, Mom's voice boomed out over the public-address system. At first I couldn't understand her words above the noise of the crowd. All around me, people were standing up, pointing at the light, trying to figure out if we were all in danger.

Then Mom's voice broke through the mounting panic. "Ladies and gentlemen," she said. "Boys and girls." It was definitely her police commander's voice. "Please don't panic. We regret that we will not be able to continue the performance tonight. Please have a safe journey home."

6 A Guilty Conscience

It's never easy to clear fifteen thousand spectators from the arena, and in this case, almost all of them were craning their necks to take one last look at the fixture on the ice rink. It's almost as if they were hoping for an even bigger disaster. Crowds can be ghouls sometimes.

I saw Mom go down to the rink and say something into her walkie-talkie. She issued an order to the security guards. "I want no one connected with the tour to leave. I'll be down to speak to them all as soon as possible."

Mom nodded to me and gave me a distracted half-smile. Then she went on the ice with the guards to examine the light fixture. Ken and Andre had both been herded to rinkside. Serge was there, too, helping both of them with their skateguards. Apparently, even in an emergency, skaters protected their blades.

"That was scary," someone whispered in my ear.

I turned to see Marc. "Wasn't it terrible?" I said. "Someone could have been killed."

Ken, Serge, and Andre were leaving the rink. "I've got to go, Marc," I whispered. "I'll see you later." I wanted to make sure that Ken was okay.

Security guards stood on either side of the entrance to the backstage areas, but I knew them both and they let me pass.

The skaters were using the large communal dressing room. Andre leaned against the wall. Ken slumped down on a chair. "Kelly!" he exclaimed when he saw me. "Things certainly happen when you're around."

"This is no joking manner," said Serge.

"Matter," corrected Ken.

"I don't see how you make jokes about this," insisted Serge. "It could have been fatal."

"It was an accident," said Ken. "I'm fine. I don't know why everybody is so excited. Accidents happen."

He slipped off his skates, revealing a thin pair of silk socks that were drenched with perspiration. When he took off his socks, I gasped in horror. Two of his toenails were completely black. The other toes were so misshapen that they looked like tiny hammers. His feet looked as if they belonged to an alien, not a human being. The tendons on his ankles were as thick as a lighting cable.

Ken caught me staring at his feet. "Never seen a skater's feet before?" he asked. He took out a jar of powerful-smelling liniment and rubbed it on his ankle and foot. "Old problem," he said. "Weak left ankle."

Ken saw me turn away. "Which is worse, the look of my feet or the smell of this ointment? You should have seen my feet when I first started out. They looked like something that had gone through the shredder, eh, Serge?"

Serge wasn't thinking about Ken's feet. His lips were tightly pursed. "I don't understand it," he muttered. "It is getting impossible. One thing right after another. Where will it end?"

Andre hadn't said a word since he had entered the dressing room. Ken looked up at him. "You okay, Andre?"

Andre didn't answer him at first. "Okay . . . if you call almost being killed okay."

"Andre, you've had a terrible scare," said Serge. "Come sit."

"I want to get out of here," said Andre.

Serge stood up and offered Andre his seat. Finally, Andre sat down opposite Ken.

"Man, flying light fixtures . . . just what we needed as a finale," said Ken. "It scared the living daylights out of me, if you know what I mean. Get it? Living daylights."

Andre glared at him. "Stop being an idiot, Swanson."

"Me . . . well, sorry. I know I'm supposed to be cool when a point almost hits me on the head."

"Ken, Andre," said Serge. "You both have reason to be upset. Don't take it out on each other. I'm sure Kelly's mother is investigating the accident right now."

"I was the one in danger," said Andre. "Ken was finished. It fell closer to me." He took off his skates. His feet were every bit as mangled-looking as Ken's. Serge handed him his shoes.

"I was sorry I didn't get a chance to see you skate," I said to Andre. "Maybe tomorrow night."

"Yeah, your friend Ken's very sorry, too," said Andre.

Just then Mrs. Clifton burst through the door. There was hardly room for her and her fur coat. She turned and glared at the security guards at the door.

"They had the nerve to try to keep me out. Luckily, I had that stupid pass you gave me, Serge."

"The backstage passes are for the performers' safety," I muttered.

Mrs. Clifton ignored me. "Andre, my dear, you must have been so frightened."

"What about me?" Ken asked.

Mrs. Clifton looked at Ken. "It fell much closer to poor Andre," she said.

"That's for sure," said Andre.

"This is not helpful," said Serge. "What matters is *why* it fell. And what matters most is that no one was hurt."

Mrs. Clifton gave Serge a dirty look, as if she was the only one who could decide what was important.

"I think we should go straight back to the hotel," she said.

"That's what I want to do," said Andre.

"No one will go anywhere," said Serge, "until we hear that it is safe."

There was a discreet cough of agreement from one of the guards. "Ms. Ross would like you all to stay here until she can talk to you," he said. "She particularly wants to speak to Mr. Emerson and Mr. Swanson."

Nobody said anything for several seconds. Finally, there was an electrical cackle on the guard's walkie-talkie.

I could hear my mother's voice through the static, but I couldn't make out the words.

The guard pushed a button and put the walkie-talkie back on his belt.

"Ms. Ross would like you all to go to the conference room," he said.

With one guard leading the way and another behind us, we walked down the corridor toward the staff elevator. No one said a word. The heavy breathing sound of the ice compressor seemed to bounce off the walls. The compressor is the machine that lowers air temperature in the pipes beneath the rink to keep the ice frozen. It works in cycles and when it's on, it sounds like the Phantom of the Dome.

I shuddered.

"Are you all right?" Ken asked.

"I guess I'm just jumpy. That sound startled me."

Andre glanced toward the compressor room. "That's one sound we're used to," he said.

We reached the elevator. The head of maintenance was coming out as we were going in. Marc was with him. Marc's head was down and he didn't see me.

"Marc?" I called.

Marc jerked his head up, and then quickly looked away. I was worried. I wondered why Marc looked so upset.

We took the elevator upstairs and filed into the conference room next to Watson's office. Watson Dellinger was at Mom's side. He greeted Mrs. Clifton warmly. She sat down next to him as if she was in charge.

"Please, sit down," said Mom to the others. "I asked you to stay because both Ken and Andre were on the ice at the time of the accident."

"I want to apologize on behalf of the Dome for

the accident," said Watson. "I'm just so glad that no one was hurt. I'm sorry, Mr. Emerson, that we had to cancel your performance."

"You realize it was out of concern for your safety," added my mom.

Andre nodded.

Mom continued. "I've interviewed the maintenance staff. The light was checked this afternoon, as it is before all performances. It was in perfect working order, yet somehow a cable snapped. I've examined the cable and it doesn't look tampered with. It seems unlikely that it could have been timed to fall when it did. I assume it was an accident. But I don't think we can rule out sabotage—not yet. Now, you may not know it, but the Dome has an unusual security system. All the services are coded so that only someone intimately connected with the Dome would even know how to find the lighting booth."

Ken and I glanced at each other. I wondered if Mom already knew about our visit to the lighting booth. Maybe that's why Marc had looked so upset. Surely Mom wouldn't think any of us had fooled with the light fixture.

Ken leaned forward and whispered into my ear. "I need to talk to you and your mom alone," he hissed.

I looked up at him, startled.

Watson coughed. "I wanted to know how you feel about performing tomorrow night. I don't think we should overreact. I know skaters. You're tough. Since you are the stars involved, I thought it should be discussed with you and Serge."

"I certainly want to skate tomorrow night," said Andre.

"Me, too," said Ken. "Nothing personal, Andre, but I don't need a convenient accident to beat you in New York."

"We'll see," said Andre.

"I am not at all sure they should skate," said Serge. "I have been in skating arenas where they have thrown glass bottles at skaters, but never a lighting fixture."

"We're having the fixture lowered and removed by the maintenance crew," said Mom. "If the skaters perform tomorrow, it will not be hanging over them."

"What will light their performance?" asked Serge.

"We have banks of regular arena lights to light the ice rink," said Mom.

Serge sighed. "My heart is worried, but my mind says that we should not cancel—not in New York. You both need the practice of working under pressure."

Ken laughed. "Well, you certainly can call flying light fixtures pressure."

The others looked at him as if he had made a bad joke.

"I think we should not cancel," said Serge finally.

"That settles it for me," said Andre. "I'll definitely perform tomorrow. Ken, if you want to back out, say so."

"No way," said Ken, but he was looking at the floor.

Serge and Mrs. Clifton stood up. "All right, let us all go back to the hotel," said Serge.

"Come on, Ken," said Mrs. Clifton.

Ken shook his head. "Uh, I'd like to stay. I sort of want to talk to Ms. Ross alone."

"What?" exclaimed Serge and Mrs. Clifton together.

"Uh . . . it's just that I remembered something about the mugging that I wanted to tell her about," said Ken.

"And you can't tell it in front of us?" demanded Serge.

"It's . . ." Ken stammered. He looked at me. I couldn't think of how to help him out.

"Uh . . . it has to do with Kelly," he said quickly. "She was there, too. It's just something I remembered. I need to ask Kelly a few questions privately."

Serge smiled indulgently. "I know Ken when there's a pretty girl involved," he said. "Come on, everybody. I am sure that Kelly will be quite safe with Ken. After all, her mother is head of security."

He laughed but I thought it was a pretty heavy-handed joke. But then, maybe he wasn't joking.

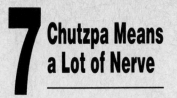

7 Chutzpa Means a Lot of Nerve

Mom asked me to take Ken to her office while she finished discussing a few details with Watson. It was past eleven o'clock. The office was empty except for Baxter, who greeted Ken with more enthusiasm than he did me. I knew Baxter was mad at me. He hated being locked up alone in Mom's office, but at least he behaved himself there. The only place he really misbehaved was at home.

"Animals are better than people, don't you think?" Ken asked.

I shook my head. "You don't have to live with Baxter. It depends on the animal and on the person."

"What could be wrong with Baxter?"

"Nothing, except if you leave him alone, he eats the furniture and pees on the floor. He almost destroyed our apartment. My bedroom door is permanently decorated with teeth marks. I'll show it to you sometime." I blushed. It sounded like more of an invitation than I'd meant, especially after Serge's crack.

Ken had the grace not to tease me. He let Baxter lick his face. Baxter kept giving me sly looks as he wagged his tail and put his two front legs on Ken's chest. It was as if he were trying to say to Ken, "Take me home with you." I knew Baxter's look— it was the one that made me take him home in the first place.

After all the excitement, it was peaceful in Mom's office. Baxter lay down at my feet. Ken slumped on the couch next to the window, looking out into the distance at the Statue of Liberty. The gold leaf of the torch winked at us.

"What do you want to talk to Mom about?" I asked. "Was it really something about the mugging?"

"No," said Ken. "I lied to be alone with you." He winked at me.

I could feel myself blushing. I hate my blushes.

"Actually, I wanted to tell your mom that I was in the lighting booth this afternoon. I figured it would be better if she heard it from me than from anyone else. But I didn't want to make a big deal of it in front of the others."

"It's just a crazy coincidence that we were in there at all," I said.

Ken didn't answer me directly. "You can't know how weird it gets on this tour," he said. "All we see is each other. From six in the morning until we're back at the hotel at night. I'm kept on a tighter leash than Baxter here."

"Actually, I don't keep Baxter on a very tight leash," I said.

"Maybe you could give Mrs. Clifton lessons on obedience training," said Ken.

"I think you're exaggerating. You're not her dog."

"Well, could you please tell her that?"

"Does she give money to Andre, too?" I asked.

Ken shook his head. "Up till now, the saintly Andre hasn't needed a patron. His parents have quite a bit of money, but even they're being stretched thin."

"I never realized how much money it took to be an amateur," I said.

Ken laughed. "Well, thanks to Mrs. Clifton, I don't have money problems."

"Mrs. Clifton sure isn't an easy person, though," I said.

Ken laughed. "That's putting it diplomatically. She liked me when I was just starting out. But lately, nothing I do pleases her. She enjoyed the 'idea' of saving me, but I don't think she likes me. She just can't seem to admit that to herself." Ken jumped up from the couch and began pacing around Mom's office. Then he stopped and said, "It's nice here. You don't suppose your mom would let me sleep here tonight, do you?"

"Here? In her office?"

Ken sighed. "I was only half-joking. But if I go back to the hotel, Serge will want to talk; Mrs. Clifton will want to talk. The only one who won't want to talk to me is Andre. And I'm not sure I want to talk to him, either."

Just then Mom came into the office. Baxter greeted her with elaborate tail wagging. She patted him on the head distractedly.

"Well, Ken, what did you want to talk about?"

"I'm scared," said Ken. "It's getting to be a little bit too much."

I looked at him. He hadn't sounded scared before.

"The mugging, even that stupid note . . . suppose somebody really is out to get me? And then it's all so insane. Kelly took me up to that lighting booth this afternoon. I was there. If Andre and Serge find out, they'll think I had something to do with it. That's why I wanted to talk to you alone."

"Hal told me that Kelly took a group of kids through the lighting booth before the performance. I didn't realize you were one of them."

"It seems like such a weird coincidence," I said.

"You know I don't trust coincidences," said Mom.

"You can trust this one," said Ken. "Kelly just happened to be telling me about the lighting controls behind door A, and I asked to see them. It's like some nightmare television quiz show. Ask the wrong question and you get accused of attempted murder."

"No one's accused you," said Mom.

"You haven't, but wait until Mrs. C hears I was there. Or Andre."

"Ken, I don't see you endangering your own life by arranging for the lighting fixture to fall so close."

"Mrs. Clifton would probably tell you it's because I have a need to fail. She's been talking that way lately. Even when I skate well, she thinks I take too many risks, and Serge half backs her up."

Ken sank down on the couch. "You saw me skate tonight. Did I look like I'm looking for an excuse to fail? She just loves doing mind tricks on me."

"Mrs. Clifton really is a piece of work, Mom." I said.

"Fortunately, that's not a security problem," said Mom. "Ken, I'm sorry for you, but I don't know what we can do to help."

Ken gave Mom an ingratiating smile. "Kelly thinks I was kidding when I asked her, but is there a chance I could just sack out in your office? I really don't want to go back to the hotel."

Mom was startled. "Excuse me, young man, but as we say in New York, you've got chutzpa."

"Chutzpa?" asked Ken.

"It's Yiddish for lots of nerve—which you've got."

"I don't have as much of that word as people think," said Ken. He absentmindedly stroked Baxter. Baxter yelped. Ken was trying to look relaxed, but I could see that his fingers had dug into Baxter's fur. "Look, Ms. Ross, I'll level with you. I'm scared to go back to the hotel. I don't want to be alone in my room. If that lighting fixture fell a few minutes earlier, I'd be dead meat."

"And if it fell a few minutes later, Mr. Emerson would be dead. For an accident, it chose a very opportune moment," said Mom.

"All I know is that I don't want to be alone," said Ken. Baxter looked up at him. "Kelly, do you rent him out as a watchdog? Baxter, would you like to be my roommate tonight?"

Baxter wagged his tail. "See, he says yes. How about it, Ms. Ross? Baxter and I will guard your office tonight."

I laughed. There was just something so appealing about Ken.

"Mom, can't he stay with us tonight? Kids are always staying at our house."

Mom looked thoughtful. "David is meeting me for a late dinner," she said. "I wouldn't mind going over this with him. It wouldn't hurt for Ken to talk with him, too."

"Who's David?" asked Ken warily.

I smiled at Ken. "A cop you'll like."

Ken raised his eyebrow.

"David's a detective at the tenth precinct," I said. "I like him a lot."

"The Dome is in the tenth precinct," said my mother. "If anything else happens while this tour is in town, he'll be involved. I'd like to get his take on this. Let me call him and see if he can meet us at home."

"Does that mean I get to go home with you?" Ken asked eagerly.

"Let me talk to Kelly alone for a minute," she said with a smile. "Excuse us. You stay with Baxter."

"Gladly," said Ken.

"Come on, Kelly," said Mom. She closed the door to the office behind her. We stood in the corridor. "He's got charm, I admit that," she said. "I wanted to make sure that you didn't just blurt out the business about having Ken stay. Do you really want him to?"

I took a deep breath. I didn't want Ken to go back to his hotel. Quite suddenly, Ken had become very important to me. I would have to talk to Chloe to figure it out. Chloe knew me better than I did when it came to boys. I wanted to fool myself into thinking that I was just trying to help Ken out—another stray, as Mom would put it.

"He really seems scared, Mom," I said. "And I like him."

"I do, too," said Mom. "But I know you, Kelly. You always want to help someone in trouble, and Ken could be trouble."

"Or someone could be trying to make it look like

61

that. Anyhow, Mom, it won't hurt anything. He'll be in the guest room. This way if something happens, we'll be right on the spot."

Mom thought for a moment. I had a feeling she was about to say no, when Mrs. Clifton came barreling down the hallway.

"I'm so glad you're still here," she said. "Ken Swanson has not returned to the hotel."

"He's still in my office," said Mom.

"He doesn't need a lawyer, does he?" asked Mrs. Clifton.

"Not at all," said my mother. "In fact, Ken asked if he could stay with us tonight. He's still upset after the accident. We have a guest room and . . ."

Ken had come out into the corridor at the sound of Mrs. Clifton's voice. "What do you mean, you want to stay with them?" asked Mrs. Clifton, interrupting Mom. She made it sound as if we lived in a roach motel.

"I just want to," said Ken softly. He sounded like a little boy.

"Mrs. Clifton," said my mother. "Surely Ken can enjoy one night in the comfort of a home instead of a hotel. Why don't you return to the hotel yourself and get a good night's sleep?"

Mrs. Clifton tried to move closer to Ken, but he did a little sidestep. "Yes, Mrs. Clifton, I'll be fine. Tell Serge that this will all work out for the best. I'll see him tomorrow morning."

"I don't think he'll approve," said Mrs. Clifton.

"He's not my nanny," said Ken angrily. "And you aren't, either." Then his tone softened. "Please, Mrs. C, it's just one night. . . ."

Mrs. Clifton adjusted the fur around her shoulders. "It is your choice, Ken. Your choice . . ."

Mother sighed. "Mrs. Clifton, let me escort you out. The Dome can be quite confusing after a performance. Kelly, why don't you and Ken meet me at the employees' entrance. I'll see Mrs. Clifton to a taxi, and then I want to go over some things with the night watch."

"The hotel we're staying at is just across the street, as I'm sure you know," said Mrs. Clifton.

"I'll see you out," said Mom decisively. Mrs. Clifton shrugged and then abruptly turned away.

Ken's eyes stayed glued to Mrs. Clifton's back until she and Mom reached the elevator. As soon as the elevator door closed, he winked at me.

I sighed. "She's a piece of work," I said.

"She just likes to make sure she's in control," said Ken. "This thing between us has been building for weeks. I'm afraid it's going to explode. Serge tells me to hang on until the Olympics. I don't think I can. Come on, let's not talk about her. I'm sick of her. Sick of talking about it. The only thing I'm not sick of lately is you."

I laughed, but nervously. I found the chaos around Ken a little scary.

"You know," I said, "I still don't understand ex-actly why you want to stay with us."

"Do you understand why you want me to?" Ken asked.

"Touché," I admitted.

Ken smiled. "I'm just trying to get to you through your dog. Isn't that right, Baxter?"

Baxter wagged his tail vigorously. There was no doubt that at least one member of our family had decided Ken could be trusted.

8 Baxter Snores

Mom met us at the employees' entrance. The streets were wet with leftover snow. Cars sped by, spitting up dirty slush. Men and women looked alike, bundled in their winter coats.

"You see more people in one night here than I used to see in a year," said Ken.

"And this is on a cold night," Mom said. "You should see it on the first warm night of spring. Everybody takes to the streets."

She took Baxter's leash from me and let him sniff at a lamp post. She and Baxter walked a few steps behind, giving Ken and me a chance to talk. Mom can be discreet when she wants to be, but she can be as bad as Chloe about pumping me for information after I've been with a guy.

"You know this is my first visit to New York," said Ken. "I thought city girls would be different. You seem much more normal than the girl who lived next door to me."

"What was she like?" I felt a little jealous.

"She spoke Norwegian, even though her grand-parents had been born here. She wanted to be a poet. She was always reading her poems to me. I think that's why we broke up."

"Because she wanted to share her poetry? That's not very nice of you."

"I didn't mind her sharing it, but it was in Norwegian. She wanted to be a best-selling poet who wrote in Norwegian. She thought it would make her unique. She wanted to be the first poet to be on the cover of *People* magazine. When I was on the cover she wrote me that she was mad that I got on first. But, of course, I had to share it with Andre. I have to share everything with Andre."

"You sound a little bitter."

"I'm not. Both Andre and I are smart enough to know that we push each other to do our best. We're just not friends, that's all."

"Were you ever? I mean, before the competition got so hot."

Ken shook his head. "We haven't known each other that long. Andre went through the juniors and seniors with no one going near him. He's an incredible technician, and I don't mean that with any disrespect. But he didn't like it when Serge took me on. In fact, he's threatened to quit Serge often, but there really isn't another coach like him. Serge's the best. So Andre threatens but never does anything about it. Andre resents any attention Serge gives me."

"And how about you? Don't you mind watching Serge work with Andre?"

"Nah, I like to work out my own routines anyhow. I pick my own music. Andre's been coached since he was six. He takes direction better than I do. Mrs. Clifton would be happier with him." Ken lightly punched my shoulder. "Hey, I get to talk about myself all the time. Let's talk about you. Like I said, you don't seem much like a New York girl."

"I'm city-born and -bred. I love the city. I wouldn't know what to do on a farm."

"There's not much to do on a farm except work. Some days I'd have to get on the tractor when it was so cold I thought I'd die. What does your dad do?"

"He's a cop, too. Only he took a job in San Francisco. A lot of New York cops were recruited to go there. I visit him in the summer."

"Boy, do you and I come from opposite ends of the world. Your dad's a cop; your mom's in security."

I laughed. "And Mom is dating a cop again—"

"What am I getting into?"

"It was your choice," I teased back. "All my friends say that being a cop is in my blood. Even my grandfather's a cop. I want to be a detective, too."

"Well, you're prettier than any of the cops I knew as a kid. I only saw them when they came to blame me for something I didn't do. I was always the first one they picked up.'"

"Why you?"

" 'Cause everyone always expected me to be trouble from the time I was born."

"No one labels a kid like that."

"You never grew up in a farm community." Ken hesitated. "Mom had me 'out of wedlock,' as they say. I guess nowadays they'd call her a single parent. My grandfather was Swedish and very strict. He let her come back to the farm to live, but he made life hell for her . . . and me. He always told me I'd end up no good. He told Mom that, too."

"She must be very proud of you now that she can prove to your grandfather he was wrong."

"She's a little jealous of Mrs. C. Mrs. C doesn't like her to come to watch me skate. She claims it makes me nervous."

"Does it?"

Ken shook his head. "No, but Mrs. C pays the money. She gets to call the shots. Mom comes to watch me sometimes anyhow. I insist on it."

"And your grandfather?"

Ken stiffened. "Now he claims that I'm just taking money from a wealthy woman, and I'm still no good. I can't win with him."

"But all skaters have sponsors, don't they?"

"I told you, Andre doesn't. He comes from a wealthy family. But he says that these last months before the Olympics are getting mighty expensive, even for his folks, and both of them are lawyers. I think he's looking for a sponsor."

"Would Mrs. Clifton sponsor two skaters?"

"I don't think even she's that wealthy. Besides, as she always tells me, she's throwing her heart and soul into seeing that I make the gold." Ken smiled at me. "You know, Kelly, you have a very tricky way of getting me to talk about myself instead of you. How did we get back on me?"

"Want me to quote you some of my poetry?"

"Do you write poetry?"

I shook my head. "No, I was just joking. I like to write mysteries. My teacher says we all like to write what we like to read."

"Maybe I'll read one of your mysteries someday."

"Maybe," I said.

"You're a little mysterious," said Ken.

"Me? Everyone tells me that I'm an open book. I'm a lousy poker player. I can't bluff."

"That's nice," said Ken. "It's a nice change from most of the people I'm around."

Mom and Baxter caught up with us. We don't live in the best neighborhood in the world. There are a couple of bars on the corner, and we get our share of drunks.

"I guess you don't have to worry about the streets of New York with Baxter, do you?" he asked Mom.

"Well, Kelly never walks home at night without him," said Mom. "And I like to think that what happened to you today is unusual. But I have to admit there are times when even I'm grateful for Baxter."

"Baxter's such a sweetheart," said Ken.

Mom laughed. "Kelly, you'll have to show him your bedroom door."

Ken lifted one eyebrow—something I've never been able to do. "That's the second time I've heard that. It must be something."

"My door belongs in the Dogdom Hall of Fame. Baxter's actually gnawed through it."

Baxter bounded up the stoop. Our house is a four-story brownstone. We have the top two floors, but that sounds much more grandiose than it is. Picture a dollhouse, and then raise the roof so that real people would fit into it. That will give you the scale of our house. When this house was built in the 1840s, most people were short, shorter even than I am.

The kitchen is probably the size of your closet, and my closet is probably the size of your locker at school. If a friend comes over and wants to study in my room, one of us has to sit on the bed, the other on the desk chair. There isn't room for two chairs.

I showed Ken my bedroom door. He stared at the hole where Baxter had chewed through the wood.

"Baxter, you did that?"

"Yeah—the day he did it, there was sawdust all over my room. That was when I talked Mom into letting me take him to her office on nights that I work."

Baxter lay down between us, taking up all the space on the floor. He seemed to sense we were talking about him, and I swear he looked proud of the hole in my door.

Baxter rolled over so Ken could scratch his stomach. "You're a glutton for pleasure, aren't you, boy?" Baxter's tail thumped happily on the floor.

"Come on," I said. "Let me show you where you're sleeping."

The guest room is also Mom's study, but it has a Murphy bed. A Murphy bed looks like a closet in the wall, but when you open the door, out pops the bed. Thomas Jefferson invented it first, and I've never known why they don't call it a Jefferson bed.

Ken put his gym bag down in the guest room. Baxter followed him. Baxter had definitely adopted Ken as his best friend for the month.

I heard the doorbell ring. "Kelly, Ken," Mom yelled. "David is here. Come downstairs."

"We'll be right there," I shouted. Baxter leapt ahead of us.

David stood up when I came into the room and gave me a hug. David is skinny and tall. He had acne as a kid, which left his face pitted with scars. When you first meet him, you think he's ugly, but he's the best example I know of how first impressions can be wrong.

Baxter tried to jump all over him.

"Fickle dog," said Ken. "I thought I was his favorite."

"Baxter has a 'love the one you're near' theory of romance," I said.

I introduced David to Ken. "I understand you've had a pretty adventurous day," said David.

Ken nodded. "Usually I feel it's adventure enough just trying to nail the quad and the backbend."

"You should see him skate, David," I said. "It's incredible."

"I hope to go tomorrow night," said David. "Annie's invited me."

"Officially or unofficially?" I asked.

David winked at me. "Unofficially."

"Does anyone want a cup of tea?" Mom asked, bringing in two steaming cups for herself and David.

Ken didn't want any and neither did I.

Mom curled into the big upholstered easy chair that is *her* chair. "David, there's a very strange atmosphere surrounding this tour. Ordinarily, I'd say Ken's mugging and the accident tonight couldn't be connected, but they worry me."

"I'm interested in that mugging," said David. "You didn't recognize the guy?"

"He just grabbed me from the back," said Ken. "I had on my Walkman, and then suddenly the earphones were around my neck. He was in back of me the whole time. I saw his hands, so I knew he was white, and he was wearing hightops . . . that's all I can tell you. He ran away when he heard Kelly scream. I would have, too. She sounded like a sumo wrestler."

"I don't think sumo wrestlers scream," I said.

"I meant you sounded that big."

"Mom always taught me to scream loud and deep," I said.

Mom nodded.

"A white guy wearing hightops," said David. "That's not much of a description. Did you see him, Kelly?"

"No . . . I didn't even see the hightops," I admitted. "I was daydreaming. And then I heard Baxter growl."

"We all thought that note saying I was 'to die for' was a joke," said Ken. "Then I almost was killed by that lighting fixture. Believe me, it's eerie."

David stood up. "I'll go over to the Dome tomorrow night. Annie and I will keep our eyes and ears open, and Kelly isn't a bad listener, either. You've got a pretty good team on your side. I wouldn't worry, except about making your jumps."

"If that was all I had to worry about, I'd be as happy as Baxter here," said Ken.

"He does seem to have taken a fancy to you," said Mom. "Tonight you get Baxter in your bedroom. That way you'll be safe and sound. Why don't you get some sleep? You have a big day tomorrow. Besides, I'm looking forward to seeing you and Andre go head to head. And so is half of New York."

"Good luck tomorrow, Ken," said David.

Ken and I walked up the stairs together. On the landing, Baxter stood between us as if not sure whom to follow. I felt suddenly very shy.

"Thanks, Kelly," said Ken softly.

"I haven't done anything," I said.

"You took my word," he said. "That means a lot to me. You don't know how much that means."

I smiled at him. "Sleep well, Ken." Baxter started to follow me.

"No, boy," I said. "You stay with Ken." I pointed to the guest room. Sometimes Baxter is amazingly well-behaved. He went straight to Ken's room and lay down by the bed.

"Are you sure you don't mind Baxter sleeping with me?" Ken asked.

Baxter picked his head up at the sound of his name.

I grinned at Ken. "There's something I forgot to tell you," I said. "Baxter snores."

Then I went into my room and shut the door.

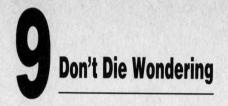

9 Don't Die Wondering

I've always been an early riser. When I was a baby, I would wake up in my crib and sing to myself at the top of my lungs. I never cried. I still wake up obnoxiously alert and happy.

This morning I could hear that somebody was up before I was. The pipes from the bathroom run right by my pillow. You can't brush your teeth in our house without my knowing it.

I looked at my clock. Five-thirty in the morning is an insane hour to be up in the middle of winter, even for me. I looked out my window. The street-lights were still on. I knew it couldn't be Mom; she is definitely a night person. So it had to be Ken.

I put on my robe. Baxter was lying down next to the closed bathroom door. He thumped his tail against the floor when he saw me, but he didn't get up. Baxter is not particularly an early-morning dog himself. I could see light streaming out underneath the bathroom door.

I dashed back into my room and brushed my hair.

This was going to be the first time in my life that I had a chance to greet a good-looking guy in my bathrobe. I didn't have to look like Dracula's bride.

I heard the bathroom door open, and then I heard someone go downstairs. I wondered what Ken was doing wandering around our house at that hour. I wouldn't look cool flying down the stairs and embarrassing the poor guy, but I was curious. Maybe he just wanted a glass of milk. The kitchen was on the lower floor. I practiced yawning in the mirror, so I could pretend that I just *happened* to be awake, too.

Finally I ventured into the hallway. The bathroom door was open and the room dark. It smelled like a locker room. The guest-room door was wide open, the Murphy bed folded back into the wall as if no one had ever been there.

I took the stairs two at a time.

Ken and Baxter were near the front door. Ken froze when he saw me. Baxter looked guilty, as if he were double-timing me with Ken.

I turned on the hall light. "Where are you going?" I asked.

"To the rink," he answered. "I was just trying to explain it to Baxter. He seems to think he's supposed to go with me."

"Why at five-thirty in the morning?"

"I have patch."

"What's patch?"

"It's a piece of ice reserved just for me. I practice my compulsory figures. I do them no matter what else is going on in my life. We all do."

"Before dawn?"

Ken reached out and ruffled my hair as if I were a little kid. "You don't know much about a skater's life," he said. "This is normal."

"It doesn't seem normal to me," I said, trying hard not to yawn for real. "Why didn't you mention this to Mom and me last night? We would have worried if we'd gotten up and you were gone. Weren't you even going to leave a note?"

Ken looked guilty. "I'm sorry," he said. "Sometimes I forget my manners."

"Don't be sarcastic."

"I'm not. It was rude." Ken looked as if he meant it. "I'm glad you're up."

"I always get up early. It's my style."

Ken smiled at me. "Want to see how boring life can be? Come watch me do my figures. It's about as exciting as watching paint dry, but it'll be an experience."

"Okay, I'm always up for an experience," I said. "As my favorite aunt always says, 'You don't want to die wondering.' "

"That's a great saying," said Ken. "Except that I would."

"Would what?"

"Like to die wondering. It'd mean that I wasn't bored. I'd like to die not bored."

"So far, after knowing you for less than twenty-four hours, I'd say that's not your problem. Life isn't boring around you."

Ken grinned at me. When he grinned, he looked like a thirteen-year-old farm boy. "You're right. Well, are you coming or not?"

"Coming," I said. "Give me a minute to get dressed, and I'll leave a message for Mom."

What do you wear at 5:30 A.M. to an ice rink? I put on my jeans. Then I grabbed my father's old sweater, the one he was going to throw out before I salvaged it. I threw on my satin Dome jacket over it all.

Baxter, who had followed me upstairs, gave me one of his mournful looks as I got dressed, as if to say, "You're going out, and it's early morning, and I have to go out, too, you know."

By the time I got to the front door, Ken was looking impatient. And I thought I had gotten dressed in record time.

"For every minute I'm late, I have to do the exercise three extra times. It's Serge's rule."

"I won't make you late," I said. "But can we take Baxter? He has to go out."

"Sure," said Ken. "I'll do a special figure eight just for him."

I scribbled a note to Mom, grabbed Baxter's leash, and we were off.

One of the homeless guys who live on our block was just getting up. The church on the corner runs a soup kitchen where they serve breakfast.

The man nodded hello to me and Baxter.

"Do you know him?" Ken asked.

"I don't know his name, but Chloe and I volunteer at the soup kitchen sometimes. It's a project sponsored by our school. He's okay. It's the crazy ones who're scary. Even the bums are scared of the crazies."

"Everyone's scared of the crazies, not just in New York," said Ken. Ken licked his lips, as if he had said too much.

We turned the corner and walked along the Hudson River. The Hudson is majestic, as wide in parts as the Mississippi. Just north of the city, it's bordered by high cliffs, and you can look out over the water and believe you are in Europe.

But here in lower midtown the land is flat, and the river laps up against the rotting piers. It is almost never pure blue. A huge tidal pull drags mud back and forth, swirling past the Statue of Liberty and Ellis Island so the river always has a brownish tinge. This early in the morning, with just a little streak of light in the east, the river looked almost black.

A concrete ribbon separates the piers from the

cars zooming up and down the street. It's a totally unplanned space, half parking lot, half joggers' lane, and we walked along it up to the Dome.

Limousine drivers who probably had been up all night parked here to eat their breakfast. Guys in trucks that sell everything from new clothes to flowers to Lord-knows-what stolen goods were setting up shop.

Ken no longer seemed in a hurry. He didn't mind when Baxter had to stop and sniff every lamp post, every pile of dirt. We walked slowly, hardly talking, but I didn't feel shy, just comfortable with Ken at my side. As we walked, the rising sun hit the top of the Dome. The Dome looked beautiful and clean compared to life on the street.

"Are you scared to go by the spot where you were mugged?" I asked. "We can take another route."

Ken shook his head. "No, I feel safe with you and Baxter as my bodyguards. Besides, I sort of like that corner. It's where we met."

I laughed. Was Ken being romantic or was he teasing me? I didn't know exactly how to act in either case. I bit my lip. I don't recommend biting your lip if a guy you like says something romantic to you. I almost choked.

"Are you okay?" Ken asked.

"Oh . . . uh . . . sure."

Ken laughed at me. I laughed back, but I didn't

have the slightest idea what we were laughing about.

We reached the Dome's employees' entrance. "Kelly, what are you doing up at dawn?" asked Stan, the senior night-security officer.

"I've come to watch Ken practice," I said.

We walked through the empty public corridors of the arena.

"My skates are in my locker," said Ken.

"I'll meet you in the arena," I told him. "I'll watch Andre until you come back."

"Tell him to wear himself out," said Ken. "I wouldn't mind it if he's not at his best tonight. He'll be gunning for me. He was furious that his performance was canceled."

I stopped at the employees' rec room and got myself a cup of coffee. I started drinking coffee a few months ago. I like the idea of drinking coffee. I think it's sophisticated. But the only way I can stand the taste is with lots of milk and sugar. "Hey, Kelly, are you getting overtime?" I heard someone say.

Marc and Tony, another maintenance worker, came in and headed for the coffee machine. "Lord, you're both here early," I said.

"We had to take apart the lighting fixture," said Marc. He patted Baxter on the head. "But we get paid for it. What are you doing here?"

"I'm a skating groupie, I guess." I giggled.

"A while ago, we were watching that Emerson guy do figures," said Tony.

"He's incredibly good." Marc sat down next to me, sipping his coffee.

Tony shrugged. "I've seen more excitement watching test patterns. First he draws circles on the ice and then he moves slow as molasses around the circle on one foot."

"That's the skill of it," said Marc.

"Well, it seemed mighty boring to me," said Tony. "Not like last night. Better watch that groupie business, Kelly."

"I'm just kidding. Ken Swanson stayed at our house last night. Baxter and I came to watch him practice."

"Ken Swanson stayed with you?" Marc asked.

I immediately felt guilty, and I had nothing to feel guilty about. "Uh . . . Mom wanted to keep him where she could watch him," I said, not exactly telling Marc the truth.

"Maybe I should get in trouble," Marc teased. "Then could I stay over?"

"Hey, we don't run a halfway house," I joked. "But you can come to dinner some time, even if you're not in trouble."

Marc blushed. "I wasn't fishing for an invitation," he said stiffly.

I felt like a clod. Maybe Marc thought I was trying to trap him into going out with me.

"I'll see you later," I said quickly, anxious to get out of there. It was confusing. I should have been comfortable with Marc and awestruck and ill at ease around Ken. Instead, it was the other way around. "Go figure," I said aloud to Baxter.

I walked through the runway down to the ice rink. The ice was empty. Baxter took the steps four at a time as we went down to the front row. I wondered where Andre was. There were only a few scratch marks on the ice, some in perfect circles. I walked around the rink to get a closer look and noticed several small, deep-looking holes near the top of each circle. I figured Andre must have been taking a break.

I enjoy the arena when it's empty. I like to fantasize that I'm a rock star about to thunder, or a circus star on a trapeze.

At the far side of the rink, I could see Ken making his way toward me on his skates and skateguards.

"Where's Andre?" he asked, looking out at the ice.

"He must have taken a break," I said. "The maintenance guys saw him."

"How about Serge? Has he turned up?"

"Nope, I'm alone. I love being the only one in the audience."

"I like having you as a public of one," said Ken, sitting down. "I guess if Serge isn't here, I can relax a minute."

"Do you want some coffee?" I offered him my cup.

Ken took a sip. "I don't really like coffee," he said.

"Neither do I," I admitted. "I just started drinking it. I thought it would make me feel grown-up."

Ken smiled at me. "So coffee's your big vice?"

"Why?" I looked at him quizzically. "You think I should be on crack? You think all New York kids are on drugs? Don't believe everything you read in the papers."

"I've learned not to believe anything I read in the paper." Ken took my hand. "Okay, my sophisticated New York girl. Come out on the ice with me. I need someone to watch the figures. Usually Serge does this for me, or Andre and I do it for each other. When I turn pro, I'll never do a compulsory figure again in my life. I curse the first guy who looked down and realized his skates were sketching a figure eight on the ice. He was probably Andre's relative."

Ken leaned down and unzipped his gym bag. "Shoot! My scribe's not here."

"I've got a pen," I said.

Ken laughed. "It's not a pen. I said 'scribe.' I

thought it was in my bag. I need one. Wait here. It must be in the dressing room."

Ken left, and I stared out at the smooth ice, fantasizing that I was Kelly Ross, skating star, the girl who could twirl on a dime and make hearts stop—particularly Ken Swanson's heart. And of course, I could skate backward like a dream.

10 Soft Ice! Danger!

Ken reappeared; his face was sunny and uncon-cerned. He had taken so long, I had begun to worry. Baxter bounded toward him across the arena, his leash slipping from my hand. Ken was carrying something that looked like a machine gun, a tube made of white metal with a black rubber handle. Short spiky blades, sharp as a razor, stuck out of one end. "Careful, boy, it's sharp," said Ken, as Baxter rushed up to smell it. Ken pushed Baxter away. Then he took off his skateguards, went out onto the ice, and skated quickly in a half-circle. Baxter tried to follow him.

"Come on," Ken said.

"Out there?" I looked at him questioningly.

"The ice doesn't bite," said Ken. "The ice is to scratch."

"Do you always talk in riddles early in the morn-ing?" I asked, as I inched across the ice in my street shoes.

"The ice is saying 'scratch me,' and I have the

right weapon." Ken slid to a stop and waited for me to catch up.

"That thing does look like a weapon. What is it?"

"It's a scribe. You'd better send Baxter back. I don't want him to get hurt."

Baxter wasn't enjoying being out on the ice anyhow. His paws splayed out in all directions when he tried to move, and he kept pausing to lick the bottoms of his feet.

"Come on, boy," I said. I picked up his leash. It wasn't easy for me to walk on the ice, either. I tied Baxter up to a railing by the seats.

Out in the center of the ice, Ken pulled out a leg from the metal tube. He stuck the sharp centering spike into the ice. He held the rubber handle and rotated the stubby downward-pointing blade. It whipped around him, etching a huge circle eighteen feet in diameter.

When the first circle was done, he carefully planted the center so that he could draw another circle just touching the first. He had a perfect figure eight.

"Your job is to see that I follow these lines exactly," he said.

I watched as Ken slowly pushed off and, following the circles, skated a perfect figure eight. He turned to study his own marks on the ice. There were only a few places where he had gone outside of the scribe's figure eight.

He frowned. "The judges mark you off for every

centimeter outside the circle, and in competition, we can't use the scribe. We have to do it from memory."

"Yours was nearly perfect," I said.

"Not good enough," said Ken.

He did it again, this time without straying outside of the lines once.

"How do you do it?" I asked. "How can you go in a perfect circle?"

Ken lifted his skate, stretching his arms out for balance. "Feel my edge."

"No thank you."

Ken laughed. "I'm not asking you to do anything dirty. Feel it."

I felt the blade. It was really two blades with a groove in between.

"We skaters worship edges. It's what makes us able to turn. Lean on one edge and you turn in one direction. Lean on the other and go the other way," said Ken. "It's that simple."

Ken pushed off on one foot, following the circles on a single blade. "How would you like your whole life dependent on figure eights?" he shouted to me. "I can hear Serge's voice in my dreams." Ken imitated Serge's clipped voice. "The crucial factor in skating good figures is control."

"I'd say right away control is not one of your strong points."

Ken made a face at me. He had shifted weight

and was moving backward, looking down at his tracings on the ice. "Control's overrated."

I heard the sharp swishing of his blade as it cut into the ice. The arena was silent except for the sound of Ken's skates. I looked up at the ceiling where the lighting fixture was gone, giving the arena a cold modern feeling. I shivered when I thought about last night's accident. The arena no longer felt like a familiar, friendly place.

"Cold?" asked Ken.

I shook my head. "Someone just walked over my grave. That's what my grandmother says happens when you shiver with no reason."

I shivered again. "What's wrong?" asked Ken sharply. He was still skating around me in circles.

"Nothing." I watched Ken. In truth, he was very much in control. He was someone who was used to flirting all the time, used to getting his own way.

I must have trembled again without realizing it. Ken stopped and put his arm around me. "You're cold. You go sit with Baxter if you want."

"I'm fine," I said; but I must have bitten off the words the way I do when I'm upset.

"You don't sound fine," said Ken. "You sound worried. That's the nice thing about skating. You don't think, you just do. You worry too much."

"Maybe you don't worry enough," I said.

Ken pushed off again, this time starting his figure with his back to the center. He looked at his tracings on the ice. "I shouldn't worry. These figures are good. I wish Serge were here. Or even Andre. Andre'd be worried. He doesn't like it when I don't muck up my figures. He likes to feel superior."

"That's what I could never do," I said.

"What? Feel superior?"

"No, skate backward."

Ken laughed at me. "You must have quit too early. Skating backward's as easy as skating forward."

"I tried. Now who's acting superior?"

"Someday, I'll teach you to skate backward," said Ken. "It's a promise. I always keep my promises." Ken shifted his weight again. "I'm doing an inside rocker, by the way."

Ken was good. I knew he didn't hate making figures as much as he claimed. He seemed to enjoy showing off in front of me, and he liked being able to explain what he was doing.

Ken finished one circle. His free leg kicked out at a right angle. Then the edge of his blade stuck in the ice. He slipped and fell hard on his side.

He swore. I shuffled over to him, walking awkwardly on the ice. "Are you all right?"

Ken stood up. "This ice stinks," he said, swearing again.

"Hey, cool down. This can't be the first time you've fallen."

Ken brushed the ice from his jeans.

"It's the millionth, but this is supposed to be a professional ice rink. Look at that." He dug his toepick into the ice. Water splashed up. "It's mush! It's disgusting."

I felt as if he were attacking me, not the ice. "So the ice is soft here. It's just a mushy spot."

"Just a mushy spot—could've been the end of my career," snapped Ken. "I know a skater who broke his tibia and fibula straight through. His leg went in one direction and his foot in another. He was doing his figures slowly, like me . . . and he hit a soft spot."

Ken's fury was scary. He glared down the far corner of the rink. "Look at that. Another puddle."

I shuffled over, slipping and sliding all the way, trying hard not to step on any of Ken's tracing. Ken was right. A film of water was forming on top of the figures that Andre must have scratched on the ice.

"This definitely doesn't look right," I admitted.

"The compressor must be off," Ken said. "I'll check it."

"The maintenance guys are around. I'll go get them."

"Tell them to meet me there. I was raised next to a compressor. Every kid who plays hockey knows how to fix one. They're all the same."

Ken shot past me on his skates without waiting

for me. He put on his skateguards and was headed out of the arena.

"Wait!" I shouted to his back.

I tried to run on the ice, but I kept slipping.

When I finally reached the edge of the rink, Ken was nowhere in sight. Baxter was barking. I untied him and went to the staff room, but Marc and Tony weren't there. Maybe they knew something was wrong and were already working in the compressor room.

I went down the corridor, past the dressing rooms. I could hear the sound of the compressor as it made loud, rhythmic, bellowing noises. The door to the room was open a crack.

"Ken?" I called.

No one answered.

11 Too Many Coincidences

I pushed open the door to the compressor room. Ken was staring at me. He was holding the telescoped leg of a scribe. The blade of the scribe was bright red.

Baxter started whimpering. I looked down at the floor and saw Andre Emerson, lying still. I screamed.

Ken dropped the scribe and fell to his knees. He lifted Andre's head and cradled it in his lap. I could see blood matted on Andre's hair. His chest was moving up and down.

"Don't," I shouted. "You're not supposed to move him, especially his neck. Thank God, he's alive."

Ken swallowed hard. Gently, he lowered Andre's head back down.

"I'll get help," I said. I ran to the nearest security phone and yelled into it. "Get an ambulance. We have an accident in the compressor room."

"Who is this?" asked the voice.

"It's Kelly Ross!" I shouted. "Hurry!" I hung up the phone and ran back to Ken.

Security moved fast. Stan, the entrance guard, met me in the compressor room. He pushed Ken away and examined Andre.

"He's got a lump on the back of his head as big as an egg," said Stan. "What happened, Kelly?"

I told Stan the little I knew.

Andre began to groan. "Take it easy," said Stan. "You're okay."

The emergency medical team arrived just minutes later. Ken and I stood to the side as Andre was lifted onto a gurney and carried to the ambulance.

Stan followed them out. "I called your mother," he said to me. "You two stay here and wait for her. Don't touch anything."

Ken's eyes followed the gurney until it disappeared out a passageway.

"He'll be okay," I said to Ken.

Ken blinked his eyes. "I can't believe it," he muttered. "I can't believe it."

"Ken, did you see anybody? What happened?"

Ken turned on me angrily. "How would I know what happened? I know nothing! Nothing!" His voice echoed in the corridor.

"Don't shout at me," I said softly. "I'm on your side."

"Yeah, but for how long?" mumbled Ken. He ran his hand through his long hair. "This is a nightmare."

I couldn't think of anything else to say. Ken had summed it up.

Mom arrived minutes later. She gave me a quick hug as she listened to Stan tell her what had happened. "Kelly, you and Ken stay here," she said. Then she and Stan went into the compressor room.

"They're going to think I did it," muttered Ken.

"No, they won't," I said; but my voice was shaky. "Why would you attack Andre?"

Ken laughed, a little hysterically. "Why? Can't you see the headlines: EX-CON SKATER COULDN'T TAKE THE PRESSURE. One more story about how 'rehabilitation' doesn't work."

"Ken, Mom doesn't believe that," I argued.

"Well, you wait, Kelly. When it all sinks in, you'll think that way, too," said Ken.

"Stop worrying about yourself for a minute, will you?" I snapped. "What about Andre, for heaven's sake? Or think about me. It was scary for me, too."

Ken's face lost its angry expression. "I'm sorry, Kelly. I'm sorry I dragged you into all this."

"You don't have to be sorry," I said. "Just don't sink into that 'poor me, everyone's against me' nonsense, okay?"

Ken laughed "You're right."

Mom came back at that moment. "I've called David at the precinct. He'll be here shortly. Ken, first I want to talk to Kelly alone. I'd like you to stay with Stan."

Mom's voice was polite, but Ken's eyes bored into me. He and I both knew he was being held under guard.

Mom took Baxter and me to her office.

"Are you all right?" she asked when we were alone.

"Yes," I said softly. "Do you think Andre will be all right?"

"Stan tells me that Andre was beginning to regain consciousness by the time the ambulance came. That's a good sign. Kelly, I want you to tell me everything you know."

"Ken and I never saw Andre until Ken found him in the compressor room. Marc and Tony saw him, though."

"I know. I'm going to question them next."

"We knew Andre had been there," I continued. "We could see scratch marks on the rink. Ken started to skate, to do his figures, but the ice was soft. He wanted to check the compressor. I told him he shouldn't look at it himself, but he was impatient . . . he . . . he . . ."

"It's okay, Kelly," said Mom. "Take a few deep breaths. You're doing fine. Just tell me slowly."

"He knew where the compressor room is because it's right near the dressing room. You can't help but hear it."

"I know," said Mom. "It's a design flaw. The architect didn't realize how noisy compressors are."

"I went back to the staff room to see if I could find Marc and Tony. Nobody was there. Then I tried to find Ken. I went to the compressor room and that's when he . . . I mean . . . we found Andre."

"Which was it, Kelly?" Mom asked gently. She had picked up what I had been afraid to say out loud. "You weren't with Ken when he found Andre, were you?"

I shook my head no.

"How long was Ken alone?"

"It wasn't long," I said. I swallowed hard and remembered back to earlier this morning, much earlier than the time Mom wanted to know about. I saw myself having coffee with Marc and Tony. I saw Ken leave me at the rink to get his scribe. He was gone a long time, so long that I had worried. Was it possible that he had had a fight with Andre then?

"What is it, Kelly?" asked Mom. "What's wrong?"

"Uh, Mom, this probably isn't important. I mean, I know Ken couldn't have attacked Andre. It wouldn't make sense, but . . ."

I told her about Ken's going for the scribe, and how long it took him. "But, Mom, you don't think Ken could have attacked Andre, do you? I mean, they're rivals, but somebody's attacking both of them. First Ken and now Andre. It couldn't be Ken."

"Kelly, we don't know enough to even make

98

guesses about what's happening," she said. "I just wish we knew more about that attack on Ken yesterday. I wish you had seen it more clearly."

"But it did happen," I protested.

"I know, Kelly, I know," said Mom.

"Mom," I said, "Ken thinks because of his record everyone will believe he's guilty."

"You know we don't think like that," Mom said.

"You don't," I said. "But others might . . ."

"Kelly, no one yet knows what happened. I want you and Baxter to wait here. The police will want to interview you."

"But, Mom, can I go to Ken now?"

"No, Kelly," said Mom sharply. "Not right now. We all have some questions for Ken, and he has to answer them on his own."

Mom shut the door behind her. I wanted to cry. Instead, I paced around the room, and Baxter followed me. "Baxter, you don't think Ken's a psycho, do you? We can't both be wrong about liking him."

Baxter sat down in front of me and nodded his head as if he agreed with me.

"Ken was with me almost the whole time. He was joking around. He was just gone a little while to get the . . ."

Baxter's tongue hung out as if he were waiting for my next word. I realized that if anyone came into the room, they'd think that I was totally loony.

"Scribe," I whispered to myself, remembering

Ken holding the scribe in his hand with Andre on the floor in front of him.

I sank down on Mom's couch and started to cry. I couldn't help myself.

The door opened. I expected it to be Mom or Ken. I was surprised to see Marc. "Are you okay, Kelly?" he asked. "I heard you were attacked."

"Huh? That's a crazy rumor. No, it wasn't me. It was Andre."

"Do you know who did it?" Marc asked.

I shook my head. I didn't want to tell Marc that Ken might be one of the suspects. I really didn't want to believe it myself.

Marc put his hand on my shoulder. "Kelly, if you ever need anything, you know I'm here. I was scared for you."

I managed to smile at him. "Thanks, Marc." But I couldn't tell Marc that it was Ken I was scared for.

"I've got to go," said Marc. "I just wanted to make sure you were okay. Your mom wants to talk to Tony and me."

"I think you were the last ones to see Andre before he was attacked," I said.

"We didn't really talk to him," said Marc. "We just watched him skate for a minute. Then Tony got bored."

I nodded. I really didn't feel much like talking.

Marc finally left me alone. I paced the office with

Baxter padding after me, until he got tired and just followed me with his eyes.

Finally the door opened and David poked his head inside. "Kelly?"

"David!" I exclaimed. "Mom said she called you. I guess it's your case now. How's Andre? Do you know?"

"He's at the hospital with a lump on his head and superficial cuts. We haven't been able to interview him yet, and an officer is waiting at the hospital. Now, I'm afraid I have to ask you some questions. It'll be okay, just tell me the truth."

I didn't like the implication that I would do anything else.

David asked the same questions that Mom had. He wanted me to account for every moment of Ken's time from when we left the house.

I hesitated, but I had to tell him that Ken had left me to get the scribe. I watched uneasily as David took notes.

"Where's Ken now?" I asked.

"He's with a police officer," said David.

"You haven't arrested him, have you?" I had to know.

"No," said David. He ran his hand through his hair. "Nobody's been arrested yet."

"Ken couldn't have done it," I said. "I know he's not capable of doing something like that."

"Kelly," said David softly. "You met this boy less

than twenty-four hours ago. I'm not trying to insult you. But you aren't the most objective witness. We're talking about a boy who's led quite a wild life. You can't know what makes him tick."

"Just because he isn't squeaky clean like most skaters . . ."

"Nobody's accused him of anything. However, he was there. And we've dusted the weapon, and the only fingerprints that show up are his. We're waiting to interview Andre. But certainly, Ken is not going anywhere," said David.

"Where's Mom?" I asked.

"She's notifying Watson and the others from the skating tour. By the way, you didn't see Serge Cohasset this morning, did you?"

"No. Ken expected him, but he didn't show up."

"We can't find him. He's not in his hotel room," said David. "It's curious."

David stood up. He patted me on the shoulder. "I'm sorry you got so involved in all this," he said.

I didn't want his sympathy. I wanted to know that Andre was okay, and I wanted to see Ken.

David left me alone again in Mom's office. I couldn't sit still, and even Baxter couldn't comfort me. I paced and paced. I wondered whether Ken was allowed to pace. He had so much pent-up energy. It was horrible to think of him forced to sit still, horrible to think of him confined to a cell if it ever came to that.

The door opened again, and this time Mom and David came in together. "What's happening?" I asked. "You haven't arrested Ken, have you?"

Mom sat down at her desk. "No . . . David and I want to go over your statement with you. What time did you wake up this morning?"

"Five thirty." I sat down wearily. It seemed like weeks ago. "I heard somebody in the bathroom, and I went to look," I continued. "It was Ken."

"Did you actually see him then?"

"Well, about two minutes later. He was on his way out to do his figures, and he invited me to come watch."

David leaned forward. "You walked together to the Dome—or did he go on ahead?"

"No, the three of us walked together," I said.

"Three of you?" David asked eagerly. "Who was the third one? This could be important. Can he or she verify that you were together?"

"Uh . . . I don't think so. Unless you take barks as verification. It was Baxter."

David rolled his eyes toward heaven.

"When you reached the Dome, what time was it?" Mom asked.

"It must have been about six-fifteen. I remember the sun hitting the copper on the roof of the Dome. But Stan saw us. Didn't he log us in?"

David nodded. "I just wanted to go over it with you."

"What's this all about? Why is the exact time we got to the Dome so important?"

Mom looked at David. "Is it all right to tell her?" she asked.

"Andre came to in the hospital and talked to my man," said David. "According to his testimony, he doesn't know who hit him. But he knows that the attack took place at six-ten. He was supposed to start skating at quarter to six, but the ice was soft, and he looked at his watch as he went to check the compressor. He put his scribe down to check the dials and someone hit him."

"So it couldn't have been Ken," I said excitedly. "Ken was with me."

"That's right. Except Andre says that for some reason, he thought it *was* Ken. He claims he's not trying to set him up."

"But that's impossible."

David shook his head. "Our problem is that you and Baxter are Ken's only alibi."

I must have glared at him.

"Kelly, don't give me that look. Of course, I believe you; it's just that there are a lot of things that don't make sense. I'm going down to the hospital to interview Andre myself. I'd like you and Ken to go with me. Maybe we can clear up some of the confusion."

"Mom, I'm telling the truth," I said.

"Kelly, of course you wouldn't lie about something as important as this. I just want you to be a little bit objective."

"What do you mean?" I asked in the stubborn tone I use when I know exactly what Mom means.

"I'm not talking as head of security, honey. I'm talking as your mom. I'm asking you to act responsibly. I can't go to the hospital with you. I have to go uptown. Watson insists on a private briefing on all that has happened, and then we have to figure out whether or not to cancel the performance tonight. I wish we could talk to Serge Cohasset. Anyhow, your job right now is to go with David to the hospital, but do take care."

The problem was that I did care. I cared too much.

"I'm okay, Mom. But I still think Ken didn't have anything to do with the attack on Andre."

"Leave that to the police and me," said Mom. "You take care of yourself." I got up, and Baxter started to follow me. "Baxter, you stay here," Mom said.

I went back to the outer office. Ken was ready. He wore his beige down jacket, with the hood drawn low over his eyes. David looked impatient. "Let's go, Kelly," David said. I put on my satin Dome jacket and followed. A black-and-white police car waited for us at the entrance.

12 Off the Hook

We drove downtown along the river. David rode in front with the driver. Bulletproof glass separated the front of the car from the back. A police officer sat between Ken and me in the backseat.

Ken kept his eyes straight ahead. I looked out the window, thinking about how we had walked up this same street just a few hours ago. I couldn't believe the Ken who had teased me then had anything to do with the attack on Andre.

Still, I remembered Mrs. Clifton warning me that Ken was unstable. Suppose she wasn't just a mean, possessive lady? What if she was sincere? I had been so busy disliking her that I hadn't stopped to think she might have been telling me the truth, might have felt that it really was her duty to warn me. She had known Ken a lot longer than I had.

Suppose, when Ken had gotten mugged on the street, it gave him an idea of how easy it would be to get rid of his main rival? Suppose, suppose—I decided that *suppose* was a seven-letter dirty word and pushed it from my mind.

We pulled up to St. Vincent's Hospital in front of a door marked TRIAGE. I remembered learning that word in history. It was used in World War I to separate the wounded who could be saved from those who would die.

The word chilled me. I wondered whether Andre had come close to death. Andre's room was on the top floor of the hospital. A guard stood in front of it. David flashed his identification.

"I want to talk to him alone first," said David. "Kelly, you and Ken wait out here."

Ken and I sat on the molded plastic chairs in the waiting room, across from Andre's room. Ken and I glanced at each other. It was the first time we had had a chance to be alone, but neither of us could find anything to say.

A nurse came out. "Are you two all right?" she asked. "Can I help you?"

I giggled a little hysterically. She sounded like she worked in a boutique. Can I help you? Broken bones? Heart attacks? Knife wounds?

"I'm sorry," I said. I buried my head in Ken's shoulder. I didn't know whether I was laughing or crying.

"She's okay," Ken said. "We've had a hard morning."

"I understand," said the nurse. "Who are you here to see?"

"Andre Emerson," said Ken. "Is he okay?"

"Oh yes. He's a wonderful young man. He's in fantastic shape."

"I know," said Ken dryly.

I giggled again. I couldn't help myself. The nurse finally left us alone.

Ken put his arm around me. "You okay?"

"I'm sorry . . . it's just that when she said, 'Can I help you?' she sounded like we were in a store."

Ken started laughing, too. He tried to make himself stop and ended up with the hiccups. I knew we were laughing from the tension, like making a sick joke to prove you're glad to be alive. But it felt good to be laughing with Ken. I realized that I could trust my own feelings. I knew that he hadn't attacked Andre, no matter what anybody else thought. It wasn't that I was his alibi. I was his friend.

Just then, David came out of Andre's room. Ken and I looked up as if we were caught smoking in the bathroom by the principal. "Is there something funny I missed?" David asked.

I shook my shoulders to stop from laughing, but every time I looked at Ken, he was laughing, too. It was so silly—there was nothing to laugh at, but all the tension of the morning was coming out in giggles.

"If you two can stop laughing long enough, Andre wants to see you, Ken."

Ken got serious right away. He got up stiffly. "Can Kelly go with me?" he asked.

David nodded. "I want to ask all three of you just a few more questions anyway," he said.

I didn't know what to expect when we went into the hospital room. Andre was sitting in a chair by the window. He had a small square white patch on the back of his head, and his hair had been shaved along the wound. Otherwise, he looked remarkably good.

He smiled at Ken, but it was a cool smile.

Ken swallowed. "How are you?"

"They say I've got a hard head. I gather you found me."

"You were out cold," said Ken.

"I've felt worse after bad falls," said Andre.

David watched the two competitors very closely. "Do you want to tell Ken what you told me?" David asked Andre.

"Look, I'm not accusing you of anything. I didn't see anything. But for a second when I heard someone behind me, I had the impression it was you. It was weird. I guess I was expecting either you or Serge. Serge usually meets me in the hotel lobby, but when he didn't, I figured he was already over at the Dome. He was pretty upset last night about the accident and you." Andre's eyes hadn't left Ken's face. Ken nodded.

"So I went over to the Dome myself," continued Andre, "but the maintenance guys said they hadn't seen Serge, either. I started my figures."

"I saw your marks when I got there," interjected Ken.

"Yeah, but the ice was rotten. I went to look at the compressor."

"And that's when you were attacked?" I asked. Andre nodded.

"But you just happen to remember the exact time you went into the compressor room," said David dryly.

Andre smiled at Ken. "Apparently I got you off the hook," he said. "The detective here thinks that's a little suspicious. But on the way to the compressor room, I looked at my watch. I told him I wouldn't lie to get you in jail."

"Thanks," said Ken. "I mean it. But where do you think Serge is? And what made you think it was me?"

"I wish I knew. It was just a feeling like . . . like ESP."

"Your ESP plus my fingerprints on the scribe could have landed me in jail," said Ken.

"Except that you were with Kelly," said Andre. "Anyhow, I'm sorry I even mentioned it."

110

"We're looking for anything that can link these incidents: Ken's mugging, the falling light fixture, the attack on you," said David. "You were right to tell us."

"You think there's someone in New York who doesn't like us?" asked Ken.

"That's for sure," said Andre.

The two skaters sounded more like allies than enemies. "It's getting very scary," I said.

Andre looked at me. "I don't scare easily. I want to get out of here."

"The hospital says you're okay to leave," said David. "But you're to go back to the hotel and rest."

"I intend to skate tonight," said Andre.

"Are you nuts?" I exclaimed.

Ken guffawed. "All skaters are nuts."

"I don't know about skating so soon," said David. "You'll have to talk that over with the doctor who's going to check you out."

"I've skated after worse injuries than this," said Andre.

"What about me?" Ken asked. "Am I free to go?"

David nodded toward Andre. "Andre sticks to his story, so you're in the clear."

"I told you," said Andre. "It's no story. I know what time it happened, that's all."

David sighed. "I have to be going myself. Andre, is there anyone you want me to call?"

"Serge," said Andre. "But the nurses have been trying him since I got here, and he's not in his hotel room."

"How about your parents?" asked David.

"No," said Andre sharply. "I don't want them flying in from California. I'll call them myself, later."

"I think some adult should be notified," said David.

"I'm twenty-one," said Andre. "Last time I looked, that made me an adult."

"I want both you and Ken to be careful," said David. "We don't want any more incidents while you're in New York."

"Do you think I like getting my head bashed in?" asked Andre. "I'm not that much of a hardhead. It hurts."

David got up to leave just as the door to Andre's hospital room was shoved partway open and then shut again.

"What do you mean I can't go in there?" asked a shrill voice. "I must see that the boy is all right. I just heard of that terrible accident."

Andre groaned. "Mrs. C . . ."

"I am sorry, ma'am." We could hear the guard's raised voice from the other side of the door. "He has visitors right now."

"You'd better let her in, Andre," warned Ken. "She won't stop shouting until you do."

"Who is she?" asked David.

"She's my patron," said Ken. "Lord knows what she's doing here to see Andre." Ken turned to Andre. "You didn't call her, did you?"

"No, but she's been hanging around me lately. I don't know why. You're right, she won't go until I see her."

David went to the door. "You can come in," he said politely. "I'm just leaving."

Mrs. Clifton barreled past him as if she expected to be trampled by hordes of police officers. She stopped short when she saw me. "What is *she* doing here?" she demanded.

"She came with me," said Ken.

"Ken, I'm surprised to see you here. I'm afraid I heard that you were under suspicion. Andre, my dear, are you all right? I was so worried about you."

"I'm okay," said Andre. "I just had a scare. And Ken is not under suspicion. He couldn't have done it. He was with Kelly."

"How convenient," said Mrs. Clifton.

I wanted to strangle her. What was it with this loony? She was supposed to be Ken's patron, but she was doing everything she could to implicate him. And just a while ago, I was telling myself that I might be wrong about her.

"I've always said New York City is dangerous, and this proves it," said Mrs. Clifton. "I used to live here. I'm glad I moved out. It's an absolute jungle today."

I hate it when people call my hometown a jungle. I don't go around putting down other cities.

"Andre, is there anything you need?" Mrs. Clifton asked.

"A little peace and quiet," said Andre. "I want to go back to bed."

He gingerly rose from his chair. Mrs. Clifton tried to help but only got in the way. Andre got into bed and pulled the covers around him. "I'm going to take a nap until I talk to the doctor about skating tonight."

"Do you want me to sit with you?" Mrs. Clifton asked.

"Please, no," said Andre. "I'll be fine. The nurses are very nice. Just ask Serge to call me when you see him."

"I won't leave you alone," said Mrs. Clifton. "I'll just ask the nurses when you can expect the doctor." She tiptoed out of the room, saying, "I'll be right back." She made it sound like a curse.

"I wish I could tell the guard not to let her back in," Andre muttered to Ken.

"You rest. I'll take care of Mrs. C. At least she doesn't feel she owns you."

"Yeah, but she's trying," said Andre sleepily.

"Get better, Andre." Ken got to his feet. "I want to settle this stuff on the ice."

"I told them you were too cocky to hit me over the head," said Andre. "You're enough of a jerk to think you can beat me. Anyhow, with any luck I'll be there tonight. Now get out of here."

We left the room. Unfortunately, Mrs. Clifton was waiting for Ken.

"Such a tragedy," she said. "He's such a fine young man."

"He's going to be okay, Mrs. C," said Ken. "Don't worry. We'll be going head to head again soon, and your investment is safe with me. I can still beat him."

Mrs. Clifton frowned. "How can you think of money and investments at a time like this? We must worry about Andre's safety." She paused. "And yours, of course."

Mrs. Clifton settled herself on one of the orange plastic chairs. "The doctor hasn't even begun his rounds. Weekends in a hospital are always so tiresome."

"Mrs. C," said Ken, "why don't you go back to the hotel? Andre will be there soon."

Mrs. Clifton looked as if she couldn't make up her mind. Then she abruptly stood up. "Come back with me to the hotel, Ken. We have a lot to talk about."

Ken surprised me. Very gracefully, he kissed Mrs. Clifton on the cheek. "I'm so sorry. But Kelly and I have something to do."

He took Mrs. Clifton by the elbow and escorted her out of the hospital. She was still protesting when he hailed a taxi for her and helped her into it. He gave the driver the name of the hotel.

Then he grabbed my hand. "What do we have to do?" I asked.

"Nothing!" shouted Ken joyously. "That's the beauty of it."

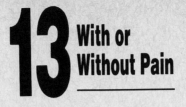

13 With or Without Pain

Ken took a deep breath. "Do you realize this is the first moment we've been free since early this morning?"

"It feels like it's been a month. Do you want to take a taxi to your hotel?"

"Where are we?" asked Ken, ignoring my question. We were at Twelfth Street and Seventh Avenue.

"We're in the heart of Greenwich Village," I answered.

Ken jumped on his toes. Other people might show their excitement in their eyes. Ken's got translated right away to his feet.

"Let's wander!" he exclaimed.

"Wait a minute," I said. "We've been up since five-thirty A.M."

"Kelly, please. If I go back to the hotel, do you know what'll happen? Mrs. Clifton will want to talk. You wouldn't wish that on me."

"What about Serge?" I asked.

117

Ken came down on his heels flat-footed. "What *about* Serge?" he echoed.

"Shouldn't we stay to find out where he is?"

Ken got a stubborn look on his face. "All right. There's a phone. I'll try him at the hotel."

We had to try three different street corners before we could find a phone that worked. Ken had to borrow a quarter from me to make the phone call. I could hear Ken talking in the receiver, but I couldn't make out the words above the noise of the traffic.

Ken hung up. "Did you talk to him?" I asked.

"No, he's still not there. If he can take off, so can we." Ken grinned at me. "Nothing's stopping us."

Ken looked through a chain-link fence into a playground where hundreds of merchants were selling their wares. "What's going on?" he asked. "Is it a street fair?"

I looked around. We were on Greenwich Avenue. "Wrong season. It's just a flea market. It goes on in this school playground all year on Saturdays. Do you need any old clothes? Junk jewelry? A toaster?"

Ken shook his head. "Let's just walk a little. You can show me around. I know you. You love to show off New York. You know it better than anyone I've ever met."

Ken looked so eager, he was irresistible. "All right," I said. "You get Kelly Ross's grand tour. But

I gotta warn you. I love history. Some of my friends say that I'm a bore."

"A day off in New York—with you? Don't worry, I won't be bored. I won't die wondering. Besides, after last night and this morning, I wouldn't mind being a little bored."

We walked down Greenwich Avenue to Washington Square Park. Greenwich Village wakes up later than the rest of the city, and the park was pretty quiet, except for the runners jogging around the perimeter.

A kid in a bundled-up jacket whispered, "Loose joints."

I laughed. "He's admiring the way you move," I said to Ken. "Get it? He thinks you have loose joints."

Ken stared at me. "You're teasing me," he said. "He's selling dope." I grabbed Ken's arm as we walked toward the fountain.

The kid selling marijuana might not have been admiring Ken's loose joints, but it was true that Ken was the most graceful walking companion I've ever had. He almost floated above the sidewalk in a peculiar half-stride, up on the balls of his feet.

Here on the streets, it felt as if we had left the tour, with its terror and tension, far, far away. Ken smiled at me. "Isn't it great to be alone?" he said.

"We're surrounded by about a million people," I reminded him.

"I know. But we don't know any of them," he said. "That's what's so great about New York."

"I was sort of thinking the same thing," I admitted.

"I like being with you, Kelly," said Ken.

I wasn't sure how to answer. Lord knows, I liked being with him, too, but he was scary. As usual, when in doubt, I babbled.

"See that tree?" I pointed to a huge oak. "It's over two hundred years old. In Colonial times, they hanged people from that tree. They executed a woman named Rose Butler just because she stole something. People used to come to watch."

Ken studied the tree. "People would probably still go to an execution if they could. Probably half the audience at the Dome tonight will be there to see if another disaster happens."

I sat down on one of the benches in Washington Square. My good mood just seeped out of me. I felt tired and sad, but I couldn't exactly tell you why.

Ken sat down next to me, his shoulders slumped.

"We can't stop thinking about it, can we?" he asked.

"Who do you think attacked you and Andre?" I asked. "Do you think it was the same person?"

Ken shrugged his shoulders. "I honestly don't know. Maybe it's someone who wants to hurt the tour. I can't make sense of it. Why attack Andre and me but not really hurt us?"

"Was there any hint of trouble before you got to New York?"

"Not really. Plenty of petty jealousies and fights, but nothing like this. I still feel like a suspect. Until I found skating, I didn't have anything that was good in my life. I was just reeling through space and bouncing off the walls and bouncing off people. And now it's as if someone or something is trying to take it all away from me. I know I'm the logical suspect, but I want so badly to beat Andre, to show that I can do it. I wouldn't want to knock him out so people could say I was the best by accident."

Ken took my hand and tickled my palm. It sent shivers through me. "You're a good listener, Kelly." He got up from the bench, pulling me with him. "Sorry I ran on like that. Let's go. Tell me more about Greenwich Village."

I shook my head. "Ken, we should go back. We have to at least try to find out who's doing these things."

Ken didn't let go of my hand. "Not yet . . . not yet . . . please. Come on," he teased. "Just a little more history. How do you know all this stuff?"

"Mom takes me on walking tours all over the city, and we learn about it at school."

Ken looked around him. "This city is really home to you. I never used to think of a city as being someone's home, especially someone I liked. Now New York will always remind me of you."

121

"Mrs. Clifton used to live in New York. She knows the city."

Ken smiled. "I said, 'someone I liked.' "

"Ken, if you really don't like her, do you have to take money from her? Isn't there another way for you to compete?"

Ken dropped my hand. "I thought we weren't going to talk about my problems—I want my tour guide back."

"Okay." I pointed to the fountain in the middle of the park. "They say Bob Dylan used to play here, and over there on Macdougal Street is the Café Wha. It's this tiny place, and Bruce Springsteen appeared there when he had long hair down to here." I pointed to my shoulders. "I wish I had heard him then. I worked one of his shows at the Dome, though. It was fantastic."

"You get to see a lot because of your mom's job, don't you?"

"Yeah, I'm the envy of all my friends." I laughed. "It's only a little bit true. Most of my good friends work at the Dome, too."

"You know what I like about you?" Ken said.

I held my breath. Was it going to be my red hair? My eyes? My short legs? Maybe just the whole of me.

"You move around the city as if no one is going to hurt you," Ken said.

I sighed. That wasn't exactly the romantic dec-
laration I was looking for. "Well, most people aren't
going to hurt you. What happened to you yesterday
and what happened to Andre, that's never happened to me. Knock on wood." I rapped my knuckles on a ginkgo tree.

I took Ken's hand. "Come on, I'll show you
something secret."

We ran across the street and up Fifth Avenue.
Ken was like a little kid. We both knew that we
were playing, pretending that the nightmare of the
attacks wasn't real. We were out on the streets where
no one could reach us, no one could touch us. It
was a game, and I wanted to play as much as Ken.

I took him into the lobby of Two Fifth Avenue.
It's a big white apartment house that doesn't look
special at all, except that in the middle of the lobby
you can see Minetta Brook. The stream, which flows
underground all through the Village, bubbles up
into a glass dome behind some rubber plants.

"See," I said to Ken. "This is to remind you that
we've got nature in the city, too. New York City's
built on hard rocks with streams and trees just like
anywhere else."

Ken stared into the bubbling water. "Yeah, but
in North Dakota, we don't bottle our streams."

I took Ken back across Washington Square and
over to the twisting streets of what I always think

of as the "real" Village. "Chloe's family lives around here," I said. "She's right on Waverly Place. Do you want to see if she's home?"

Ken shook his head. "No, I like it with just the two of us."

I found it a little hard to breathe after that statement.

We wandered back up Seventh Avenue, ending up close to St. Vincent's again.

"I wonder how Andre's doing," I said.

Ken started to laugh.

"What's so funny?" My stomach lurched. I didn't like to think of Ken laughing about the attack on Andre.

Ken pointed to a sign across the street: EARS PIERCED WITH OR WITHOUT PAIN.

"That sign's been there ever since I can remember," I said. "And I've always been too chicken to get my ears pierced."

Ken leered at me. "Let's do it. Which will it be . . . pain or no pain?"

"No way!"

Ken put his fingers on my neck and brushed my hair away from my ears. "You have pretty ears. You'd look good in earrings. It doesn't hurt."

"How would you know?"

Ken showed me the scar on his ear. "I had mine pierced. I liked it, but Serge made me take it out. He said it would turn off some of the more conservative judges. As soon as I turn pro, I'm putting it back in. Come on, let's get your ears pierced. It'll be my treat.''

I shook my head. Ken put his mouth to my ear. "It'll be something to remember me by," he whispered. He put his hand on my elbow and steered me inside.

The man behind the counter looked like someone left over from the sixties. He had long gray hair, past his shoulders. It was beautifully styled. It probably took him an hour to get it brushed just right. Nobody else was in the store.

"Can I help you?" he asked.

"Do you take credit cards?" Ken asked.

"Hey man, these are the eighties. Of course I take credit cards.''

"Great," said Ken. "She's getting solid-gold studs. That's so your ears don't get infected," he told me.

"I haven't said I'll do it," I argued.

Ken grinned. "Yes, you will. How do you pierce them?" he asked the man.

"The sign's a joke." He smiled at me. Actually he had a nice smile. "It won't hurt. I'll use a stud gun. It takes less than a second.''

At the word *gun*, I wanted to get out of there. "Let's see the studs," said Ken. Ken had the same intensity toward getting my ears pierced as he had in performing his figures.

I could barely look at the trays of tiny gold earrings. "You'd better find ones you like," warned the owner. "You have to keep them in for six weeks."

"Six weeks?"

"You won't feel them," Ken said. The owner winked at me.

"He's lying, isn't he?" I asked.

"You'll feel them," said the owner. "But they honestly don't hurt."

Ken held a round gold stud to my ear. "These look great. They're not too small."

"How much are they?" I asked.

"It's a present. It's rude to ask how much a present costs," said Ken.

"I can't let you buy me earrings."

"Why not?" asked the owner. "Boys have been buying girls earrings ever since I've been in business, and guys buy them for guys, and now, finally, I've had girls buy them for guys. Relax and enjoy it. Do you like the ones he's picked out?"

I nodded. I couldn't believe I was actually getting my ears pierced. The man with the gray hair led me to a high canvas director's chair facing a mirror. I looked pale.

"Shouldn't we go next door to the hospital to do this?" I joked, but I was only half-joking.

The man laughed. "You won't feel a thing. And these studs go directly into your ears. There's no danger of infection. No needles." He swabbed my ear with alcohol. Ken took my hand. The metal was cold next to my ear. I heard a click. It hurt. It felt like my ear was being squeezed between metal, which, when I thought about it, was exactly what was happening. No wonder I had put off doing it for so long.

Before I knew it, the other ear was pierced. "See? It didn't hurt," said Ken. "I told you."

"It hurt." But when I looked at myself in the mirror, I liked what I saw. The two dots of gold made me feel dressed up, a little older, and a little more feminine. I smiled. "I've got to call Chloe and tell her what I did. She won't believe it."

The man showed me his telephone, which was in the back of the store. He went up to the counter and took Ken's credit card. I dialed Chloe's number.

"Kelly, where are you?" she exclaimed. "Everybody's been looking for you."

"They haven't been looking for someone with holes in her ears," I said. Then I realized what she had said. "What do you mean, everybody's been looking for me?"

"What do you mean about holes in your ears? Are you on drugs?"

"Of course not. It's my ears. They're pierced! I did it. Ken did it for me. Who's looking for me?"

"You mean he held an ice cube to your ear and punctured it? That guy's got ice on his brain."

"We had it professionally done. You know that place, WITH OR WITHOUT PAIN. Chloe, forget about my ears. Who's looking for me—Mom? Did something else go wrong. Is Andre okay?''

"No, no, it's not an emergency. I didn't mean everybody. It's just Marc," said Chloe. I could hear her giggle. She put her hand over the receiver and shouted. "Kelly got her ears pierced. We've got to get a look at them.''

"Marc? What's he doing at your house?'' I asked.

"He wandered by. He said he was looking for you.''

"For me?''

Chloe laughed. "Hold on a minute while I go in my room.'' I heard her yell to Jesse to hang up the phone when she got to her bedroom.

"Marc rang my doorbell about fifteen minutes ago and asked where you were. He wouldn't leave. See—when it rains, it pours.''

"What're you talking about?''

"When you've got one guy, the others are all interested.''

"Chloe," I said.

She just laughed.

14 What's Playing? A Horror Show

Ken agreed to go to Chloe's with me. He seemed to be willing to do anything that didn't have to do with skating.

We walked up the four flights to Chloe's apartment. "Does everybody in New York live in places where they forgot to install the elevator?" Ken asked.

"You're in the best shape of anyone I know," I said. "You shouldn't complain."

"I wasn't complaining, just asking."

Chloe stood in the doorway of the apartment. Her dad shouted hello to me from the kitchen as I walked in.

"Let me see them!" said Chloe. She smiled at Ken. "I can't believe you got her to do it. I've been trying for years."

"They're solid gold," I said.

"That's right," said Ken. "Nobody can say that I didn't go for the gold."

Marc stood up when we entered the room. "Marc,

what's going on?" I asked him. "Did something else happen at the Dome?"

"No. But they've found a mystery guest to replace Andre, and they're going on with the show tonight."

"A what?" exclaimed Ken. Marc's eyes sparkled. I could tell he loved being the one with the news.

"Who's *they?*" I asked.

"The coach . . ."

"Serge? You talked to Serge? When?" Ken was practically shouting at Marc.

"The guy with the mustache, right?"

Ken looked as if he wanted to kill Marc. "Yes. Where did you see him?"

"At the Dome. He had seen me with Kelly yesterday, and he thought you were with her."

"I'd better call the Dome," I said. "This will clear up the mystery," I told Chloe and Jesse. "Ken has been looking for Serge since a little after six this morning."

The telephone operator at the Dome said that Mom wasn't there. Judy doesn't work on Saturdays. No one answered at home, either. I asked for the security guard. He said he didn't know where Mom was and he hadn't heard anything about a mystery guest.

"What did you learn?" Ken asked anxiously.

"Almost nothing. Marc, are you sure you've got it right?"

"I'm just a lowly maintenance guy. I'm not a skating star," said Marc. "I'm only telling you what I heard."

"What's this all about?" Chloe demanded. "You're acting like a mystery guest is the secret of the century. I think it's kind of exciting."

"Chloe, did Marc tell you what happened at the Dome this morning?" I asked.

"Another accident?" asked Jesse.

I shook my head. "Not exactly."

Marc looked uncomfortable. "I thought we were supposed to keep quiet about it. That's what the police told me."

"Telling Chloe and Jesse isn't like telling the press," I said. "Andre Emerson was attacked early this morning. Ken found him. I was there, too. It was awful, but he's okay. He's in St. Vincent's. That's why we were down in the Village."

"Who did it?" Jesse asked. His eyes darted to Ken.

"Ken was with me when Andre was atacked," I said angrily. "But if it had happened fifteen minutes later, they would have thought Ken did it. Mom had the police in. It's been some morning."

"Can I use your phone?" Ken asked Chloe. "I've got to talk to Serge. Maybe he's at the hotel. I gotta find out where he's been, and I want to find out who this mystery guest is." We heard Ken ask for Serge. Then he hung up the phone. He looked confused and a little angry.

"What now?" Marc asked sharply.

"The hotel operator said Serge wasn't there. But you're sure you saw *him* at the Dome?"

Marc nodded. "I'd know him anywhere."

"Where exactly was he when you saw him?" Ken was really cross-examining Marc.

"He was down in the dressing-room area. He looked distracted, but then he called me over and said, 'Hey, you're a friend of Kelly Ross's, aren't you?' " Marc paused and smiled at me.

"Go on," said Ken impatiently.

"He said that Kelly seemed to have kidnapped his star skater." Marc laughed. "He was joking, Kelly. But he said that nobody knew where either of you were. I said that I knew you hang out with Chloe sometimes. He asked me to try to find you and to tell Ken that there would be a mystery guest tonight."

"That's all?" Ken pressed. "He didn't say anything about the attack on Andre? Or why he didn't show up this morning for patch?"

"Hey, look, I told you—I'm just the maintenance guy. Why are you giving me the third degree?"

"Sorry," muttered Ken.

"I'll call the hospital," I said. "Maybe Serge's with Andre."

But the hospital said that Andre had been discharged.

"I'd better go up there and look for Serge my-self," Ken said.

"I thought the coach was supposed to keep *you* on a tight leash, not vice versa," said Jesse.

"It's just not like him," repeated Ken. He began to pace, but Chloe's living room was small, and it was almost as if there wasn't enough room for all of us. Marc's eyes followed Ken.

Then Marc smiled at me. I didn't want to hurt Marc. I just didn't feel the same way about him that I did about Ken. But Ken would be gone from my life very soon, and all I'd have to remember him by were the holes in my ears.

"Come on, Kelly," said Ken. "Let's get back to the Dome."

"What's your hurry?" said Marc. "You know Kelly's mom isn't there. When there's a performance at night, nobody shows up until four o'clock. There's just a skeleton crew. I was on my way to Tower Records. Want me to show you a great record store?"

Ken stared at Marc as if he were crazy. "A record store. Do you realize what I've been through this morning?"

"It's not just *a* record store," said Jesse. "It's the greatest record store in the world. It's only fifteen minutes from here. You could go there before you go to the Dome."

"I bet you could find all sorts of music for your

programs there. They have everything," said Marc.

"What do you think, Kelly?" Ken asked.

I shrugged. I understood how anxious Ken was to find Serge, but it seemed that if we rushed up to the Dome, we would just have to wait and be even more nervous.

"Let's go," said Ken.

We walked together to Tower Records. Ken and I both knew that the game we had been playing was almost over. Serge and the mystery guest just added another twist, and put more pressure on Ken. I knew Ken wouldn't feel right until he talked to Serge. I was sorry that we had even agreed to go to Tower.

The neon sign of the store beckoned us. Tower Records is like a supermarket for music. Even if you don't have any money, it's a great place to hang out. Huge video monitors are hung from the ceiling, tuned to different TV channels. They even keep one channel on the all-news station.

I took Ken into the New Music section. Marc tagged along. Chloe and Jesse went into the next room to look at jazz records.

Suddenly Ken gripped my arm. He pointed to one of the monitors. I stared. It was the all-news channel. A picture of the Dome flashed on the screen. Mrs. Clifton was giving an interview, but Tower Records never has the sound on their TVs turned on—it would compete with the music that blares continuously. Suddenly, the screen flashed to a black-and-white picture of Serge. "Why is there no sound?" Ken shouted at the monitor.

I ran to a clerk. "Is there a way you can turn on the sound?" I asked. "It's important."

The clerk pushed a button just as a reporter was saying, "The mysterious incidents at the Dome continue. Last night the lighting fixture fell, narrowly missing the United States's two top male skaters. Early this morning, according to a source close to the tour, Andre Emerson was viciously attacked, and now Serge Cohasset is missing."

"But Marc just saw him!" shouted Ken.

"Where's Marc? We'd better get up there," I said.

I looked around. Marc had been right by our side. Now I couldn't find him. I dashed around the store, but he was nowhere to be seen. "Where is he?" I demanded of Chloe and Jesse. "Is he with you?"

"Who?"

"Marc! He was the last one to see Serge. Where did he go? This is crazy."

"Kelly," cried Ken. "I've got to get up to the Dome and find out what's going on." He sounded close to hysterical.

"I'm coming," I said. I turned to Jesse and Chloe. "If you find Marc, tell him to go to the Dome right away. He may have been the last person to have seen Serge."

Jesse hailed a taxi and he and I half-shoved Ken

into it. "The Dome!" I said to the taxi driver. "Hurry!"

The taxi driver looked back at me. "What's playing there?" he asked.

I sank back into the seat and looked at Ken's white face.

"A horror show," I answered.

15 Make It Public

The Dome was under siege. Television vans surrounded it.

"I don't think we want to talk to reporters," I said to Ken. I had the taxi driver let us off at the subway because I knew I could take Ken into the Dome through the subway entrance.

A guard grabbed me. "I'm Kelly Ross," I told him. "And this is Ken Swanson, one of the skaters."

"I know," said the guard. "We have orders to escort you straight to Mr. Dellinger's office."

"Escort? I can go myself," I said.

"I'm sorry, Ms. Ross. We were told to keep an eye out for you and Mr. Swanson. I'll take you up myself."

I felt like a criminal as we silently rode the staff elevator. Ken kept nervously licking his lips.

Dellinger's office looked like a command center. Mom was clearly in charge, and she looked about as angry as I'd ever seen her. I hoped not at me.

Mrs. Clifton sat on Mom's couch, wrapped in fur. She was pale. Watson Dellinger sat next to her, holding her hand.

Andre, released from the hospital, also sat on the couch with his arms folded across his chest. The small white patch on his head was the only visible sign of his attack.

David, several other NYPD detectives, and what seemed like half of the Dome security crew were perched on every chair or leaning against every inch of available wall space.

"What's happening?" Ken demanded. "Where's Serge?"

"That's the big question," said Andre.

"Answer one question first," said David. "Where have you been since I left you at the hospital?"

"With Kelly," answered Ken.

"Well, Mrs. Clifton," snapped my mother. "That is one disappearance taken care of. Perhaps you overreacted about Serge, too."

Mrs. Clifton glared at her. "There was nothing I could do but tell the truth when those reporters asked me where Serge was. I am just one of those people who can't lie."

Mom rolled her eyes toward the ceiling. "Mrs. Clifton has alerted the press that she thinks Serge is missing," she told me.

"But Marc saw him late this morning," I said.

"Serge told Marc that a mystery skater was going to replace Andre tonight."

Mom stared at me. "Marc talked to Serge? Where is he?"

"I don't know," I said. "He was with us at Tower Records, and then he disappeared."

"Who is Marc?" Andre demanded.

"He's just a maintenance man," said Mrs. Clifton.

I stared at her. I wondered how she knew who Marc was.

Mom turned to a security man. "Ask everyone to keep a lookout for Marc Stone." Then she said, "Now, Kelly, tell me exactly what Marc said."

Ken and I took seats on the windowsill. "We ran into Marc at Chloe's," I explained. "And he said that he talked with Serge in the dressing-room area. Serge thought Ken was with me and he asked Marc to find us." I blushed. Mom was staring at me intently.

"Kelly, your ears," she said quietly.

I blushed even deeper.

"I had them pierced."

"That's the one thing that is my fault," said Ken softly.

"Never mind about her ears," said David. "I don't get why Serge talked to this maintenance guy and nobody else has seen him."

"Let's not overreact," said Mom. "Serge Cohasset's a grown man. He's been unaccounted for only this morning and afternoon. If Mrs. Clifton hadn't reported to the press that he was missing, I don't think we'd be overly concerned. Until we find Marc, I don't think we should panic."

"But what's this about a stupid mystery skater?" asked Andre. "I'm not going to be replaced by anyone. I told those doctors that I could skate."

Just then, there was a buzz from the intercom on Watson's phone. Mom pushed the button. "Yes," she said curtly. "Good, bring him in." She glanced at me sharply. "Marc Stone just showed up at the Dome. Perhaps now we can get some answers." A minute later, Marc appeared in the doorway.

"Kelly, Ken," he said. "I tried to find you at the record store, but you were gone."

Mom, however, was more interested in the fact that Marc was the only one who had seen Serge. "Marc . . . please tell me exactly when and where you saw Serge Cohasset."

Marc seemed understandably nervous. "I didn't know it was going to be such a big deal. I was cleaning out the dressing rooms. I saw him. He recognized me."

"Recognized you?" Mom asked.

"As a friend of Kelly's," said Marc quickly. "He asked me if I knew where Kelly was."

"None of this makes sense," interjected Andre. "When was this? After my accident?"

"Way after," said Marc. "After all of you had gone. About ten o'clock this morning."

"If Serge was around, he'd have come to see me in the hospital," said Andre. "He wouldn't just say to some maintenance guy, 'Oh, by the way, I have a mystery guest for tonight.' "

"Well, I'm sorry I'm not important enough for you," said Marc huffily.

"Marc, calm down," said my mother. "Now what did Serge say about a mystery guest?"

"He seemed to know about the attack on Andre," said Marc.

Mom stopped him. "How did he know about the attack on Andre if he wasn't here early this morning?"

Marc shrugged. "I don't know . . . he was just anxious to get in touch with Ken and Kelly."

"Why wouldn't he get in touch with me?" Mom asked.

"Or me?" demanded Mrs. Clifton.

Mom ran her hands through her hair. "I admit that none of this makes much sense." She turned to David. "Why don't you have somebody go down and search the dressing-room area? Maybe he left a note for Ken or Andre there."

David nodded.

"Do you need me, Ms. Ross?" Marc asked. "I'm supposed to help Tony."

"Yes, I need you," said Mom. "I don't want you to leave the Dome. Not until we find Serge."

"I'll stay right here," said Marc. "I won't leave the building."

Mom nodded and Marc left.

"Now what?" Ken asked.

"Now we wait," said my mother.

"I resent the attitude that I overreacted." Mrs. Clifton sniffed. "After all, Andre was attacked. The lighting fixture almost killed two of our skaters last night."

Ken began to pace around the room. He stopped and stared at one of the pictures on the wall. I got up and looked at it with him. I understood why it had caught his interest. It was a picture of Watson and Serge up at Lake Placid—Watson with his arm around Serge, and a group of young skaters standing behind them. One of the skaters looked familiar to me.

"Are you in that picture?" I asked Ken.

"Don't be silly. I wasn't with Serge then. This picture was taken at least five years ago. There's Andre."

Andre stood up and looked at the picture with us. "I'm always easy to spot," he said. "The only black athlete there."

"You look so young," I said. "That kid in the

back row looks like somebody I've seen before."

Suddenly there was a knock on the door.

A police officer conferred quietly with David, then handed him an envelope.

David put the envelope on Mom's desk. "They found this in the skaters' dressing room. It looks interesting."

Before Mom could read the letter, Mrs. Clifton leapt up, crossed the room, and grabbed it. Mom was so surprised she let her have the letter. Mrs. Clifton's hand shook as she read it. I realized that she was a lot older than she seemed.

"Mrs. Clifton, give that back to me," said Mom.

"It's my letter," said Mrs. Clifton softly. "This was not supposed to be public yet." I swallowed hard. For all my dislike of Mrs. C, I felt almost sorry for her. Whatever was in the letter had to be pretty embarrassing.

Mrs. Clifton looked at the letter again. "On the other hand," she said, "perhaps it does have something to do with the events of the last few days. You can read it out loud."

Mom took the letter from Mrs. Clifton and put on her reading glasses.

Mrs. C stared at Ken. "It's just as well that this is out in the open," she said. I reached over and held Ken's hand. I knew whatever was in the letter was bad news, and I no longer felt sorry for Mrs. Clifton. I had a feeling that the bad news was for Ken.

16 Curiouser and Curiouser

"My dear Serge," Mom read from the letter. "I can no longer in good conscience continue my support of Ken Swanson. As you were the one who first encouraged me to be his patron, I felt you should be the first to know of my decision to terminate this relationship." Mom paused and coughed.

We all turned to Ken. His eyes were downcast and his hand was still in mine. His nails were squeezing into my palm. Mrs. Clifton leaned against the back of the couch with her eyes closed.

Mom continued reading. "I believe in 'chemistry' and the chemistry between Ken and myself is not right. I think he is much too impulsive to make it to the top.

"I am an honest person, as you well know. I think you have made a serious mistake with Ken Swanson, but if I cannot dissuade you from continuing with him, I can certainly cut off my support. Sincerely yours, Carey Clifton."

Mom put down the letter.

"You old witch," muttered Ken. He dropped my hand.

"Ken," said my mother, sternly. "Did you know about this? Did you know she was withdrawing her support?"

"No," said Ken through tight lips. He glared at Mrs. Clifton. "You didn't say anything about it to me."

"I was going to have Serge tell you," said Mrs. Clifton. She didn't have the decency to look at Ken. "I gave him that letter last night. It is simply a matter of attitude. I don't think you have the right attitude to be a champion."

Mom and David were deep in conference. Occasionally, one or the other of them would look up at Ken.

I couldn't sit still, certainly not with Ken seething beside me. I felt as if I had memorized every picture on the walls. I walked around Mom's desk. I saw the thick gold-embossed CC on the top of Mrs. Clifton's letter.

"Can I look at this?" I asked.

Mom nodded.

I took the letter back to the windowsill and sat down next to Ken. Ken glanced at the letter, and then glared at Mrs. Clifton.

Mrs. Clifton stood up. "This is really quite embarrassing," she said. "Do you need me? I'd like to go back to my hotel."

"I would like you all to stay until we hear from Serge. He must be somewhere. This letter just deepens the mystery of why he hasn't shown up," said my mother.

Suddenly, the phone rang. Mom picked it up. She signaled to David and Watson. "One minute," she said into the receiver. "I think you should hear this," she said to David. She held her hand over the receiver. "Someone says they have information about Serge," she whispered.

She flipped on the microphone of her speaker-phone.

"*I want to speak to the head of the security at the Dome,*" said the voice.

"You're speaking to her," said Mom.

"*If you want to find Serge, go to the Hudson Line pier right now, and await further instructions. Don't take anyone with you.*" The phone clicked as the person hung up.

The voice sounded distorted. It wasn't easy to tell whether it was a man or a woman.

"What the . . . ?" exclaimed David. "Serge, kidnapped? Where did that come from? This is getting crazier and crazier."

"I told you there was something suspicious about his absence," said Mrs. Clifton, sounding pleased about the phone call.

"It sounded like a clown's voice," said Ken.

I put my finger in my mouth. "*If you want to find*

Serge . . ." I said. I sounded just like the voice. Mom and David stared at me.

"It's a trick all kids do," I explained. "It's the easiest way in the world to change your voice. You just put your thumb in your mouth and nobody recognizes you. We used to do it when we were little and made stupid phone calls. You know, calling someone and saying, 'Your refrigerator is running, you'd better catch it.' "

"I tell you, Annie," said David, "there *is* something kidlike about this. No ransom demand. And why did they want *you?*"

"They didn't want me specifically, but the security head of the Dome."

"I know," said David. "But wouldn't they ask for Watson or someone else connected with skating? It sounds like a hoax."

"Still, we have to check it out," said my mother.

"You're not going alone," argued David.

"I have to," said Mom. "You heard the person on the phone."

"I'm going to be there," insisted David. He turned to one of the plainclothes cops. "Get a wireless transistor up here right away."

"You are actually going to meet this person?" asked Mrs. Clifton. "What is to become of us?"

"You will all wait right here until we return," said my mom.

She turned back to David. "I'll wear the wireless,

and take a gun, but don't call out the S.W.A.T. teams."

"I won't," agreed David. "But we'll be close by. There may be something farcical about this, but the attack on Andre was made with a real weapon— even if in twenty years I've never heard of anyone being attacked by a scribe. It sounds like a crime in the Middle Ages in a monastery. The loony we're dealing with could be dangerous. I want you wired."

"Maybe you should take Baxter for protection," I said.

"Baxter," said my mother. "I forgot all about him. He's been in my office alone all day. He's probably destroyed it."

"I'll go get him," I said.

Mom nodded. She turned her back to us, took off her suit jacket, and put on the tiny transistor that an officer had brought up.

"I'll go with you," whispered Ken. Mom was busy with David. Ken and I slipped out into the corridor and went down to Mom's office. As Alice in Wonderland might say, this truly was getting curiouser and curiouser.

17 Mohawk A Razor Camel

Baxter was ecstatic to see us. He wagged his tail and jumped all over me. He slobbered on the expensive paper in my hand. I pulled it away. I hadn't realized that I was still holding Mrs. Clifton's letter.

Baxter turned his attention to Ken. "At least he's happy to see me," said Ken. "Baxter, you wouldn't like to be a patron, would you?"

"I'm sure he'd love it," I said.

"I think he needs to go out," said Ken. Baxter was whining and jumping toward the door.

"We'd better ask Mom if we can take him out, or get a guard to," I said. I placed Mrs. Clifton's letter on Mom's desk and tossed Baxter's leash to Ken. He snapped it on.

I was exhausted. I was in no hurry to go back to Watson's office and Mrs. Clifton. At least taking Baxter out would give me an excuse to get some air.

I glanced at the back of the letter.

"Mohawk A Razor Camel," I read out loud.

"What!" exclaimed Ken. "Say that again."

" 'Mohawk A Razor Camel'—it's written on the back of her letter. Aren't those skating terms?"

"Let me see that," said Ken.

I handed the letter to him. "That's Serge's handwriting, not Mrs. Clifton's," said Ken. "Mohawk A Razor Camel?"

"Is that a new move?" I asked.

"No . . . it'd be impossible. MRC? Marc?"

"What about Marc?"

"I don't know," said Ken. "But Serge always gives his skaters a silly code name made up of skating terms. It's one of his little games. You just read the first letters of each word. *Mohawk* is an easy jump. A *camel* is a layback."

"I don't need a lecture on skating terms," I snapped. "Why would Serge have a code name for Marc?"

"You got me," said Ken.

"You know, Marc is right in the middle of things," I said. "He's the only one who saw Serge."

"Oh, no," said Ken. "I should have thought of this earlier. There was a Marc who used to skate with Serge. He got dropped. . . ."

"Remember that picture?" I broke in excitedly. "I said one of the skaters was familiar. It could have been Marc. And Marc seemed to know a lot about figure skating. Come on. We've got to tell Mom and David. They could be walking into a trap."

150

We ran out into the hallway with Baxter on his leash.

Mrs. Clifton and Andre were alone in Dellinger's office. "Has she gone?" I asked.

"They left several minutes ago," said Andre. "All the police officers went with her."

"What about the Dome's security officers?" I asked.

Andre shrugged. "A couple of them went with your mother. We're supposed to wait here until they get back."

"And Watson?" I asked. "Mr. Dellinger?"

"He insisted on going, too," said Mrs. Clifton.

"Hurry," I said to Ken. "We can notify one of the guards downstairs." We went back out into the hallway. Ken pushed the button for the staff elevator. I grabbed his hand. "We'll lose too much time. Those elevators are always slow."

We ran down the curved hallway. We were almost at street level when Ken grabbed me and pushed me against the wall into a recess for one of the concession stands. He put his hand over my mouth.

Footsteps were coming down the hallway in our direction.

"It's Marc," Ken whispered. "I saw him coming through the door."

"Shh," I warned. We backed up farther against the steel gate that kept the concession stand locked.

"We can't let him spot us," Ken whispered. I

pointed toward an open doorway marked *B*. We slipped through the door and shut it behind us.

"What does *B* stand for?" Ken muttered.

"Basketball," I said. "It's where they store the basketball court. It's one of the few signs that makes sense."

The basketball court comes apart like a giant jigsaw puzzle. It can fit right on top of the rink. When it's pulled apart, the wooden parquet floor is stored in a small area in neat piles, each over six feet tall.

Suddenly, the door to the storage area opened. I shoved Ken into one of the narrow corridors between two stacks of wood. I tried to make my breathing as quiet as possible. I tightened up on Baxter's leash and put my hand over his muzzle. We could hear Marc moving around.

"Anybody there?" he called.

Ken and I both held our breath. I got down on the floor, flat on my belly. "Drop dead," I hissed at Baxter. It was one of the only two things he had ever learned at obedience school—to play dead on command. He lay down without a sound. I thanked goodness for his obedience training. I peered around the stack of wood.

Marc was sitting on part of the basketball court, pulling on a pair of skates. Then he stood up in his skateguards, his shadow falling against the wall, and picked up a gun.

I was trying to inch back toward Ken when I

rolled on top of something warm that felt like a snake. I almost screamed.

Then I heard the door open and Marc left.

I got to my feet. Under my stomach was a piece of rope. I held it in my hand.

Ken stared at me in confusion. "What's going on?" he asked.

I tiptoed to the door and peered out into the hallway. There was no sign of Marc. But it didn't matter. There was only one place where he could be going in skates. I just didn't know what he was planning to do when he got there.

18 Play Dead on the Ice

The arena lights were dim. Out in the center of the rink, I could see a skater moving in slow warm-up circles. I inched my way around the rink, holding tight to Baxter's leash. I held my finger to my lips, warning Ken to keep quiet.

A lone figure sat stiffly in the judges' box, empty seats on either side of him.

"You'll see," shouted the skater. "I've been practicing. I've been lifting weights. I'm better now than I ever was. I just want a last chance to skate. I'm going to prove to you that you were wrong."

"Untie me and I'll watch," said the man in the judges' box. "You untied my legs to move me here. Now untie my arms and this rope around the chair, and I'll watch you skate. I'll help you, the way I used to."

"Serge!" whispered Ken.

"Shh," I warned him.

"If I untie you, you'll run," said Marc, practically

sobbing. "It's too late to let me be a mystery guest. It's all gone wrong. But I'll show you. . . . I'll show you. . . ."

"Marc," shouted Serge. "It's not too late to stop this foolishness."

"Yes, it is!" snapped Marc. He pulled out the gun from under his satin jacket. "They'll be back soon. But you're going to see how good I really am."

"I'm going to get help," I whispered. I turned to leave, and as I did, I stepped on Baxter's tail. He yelped.

"Who's there?" shouted Marc. "Come out, or I'll kill him now."

"Ken," I said. "Go get Mom. I'll stall him. Marc won't kill me."

"Kelly, he's insane," Ken whispered urgently. "Don't . . ."

"Get help!" I insisted.

Still holding Baxter by his leash, I stepped gingerly onto the ice. The gun that Marc was carrying had a small caliber. He'd have to get very close to hit me, and he wouldn't be able to keep both Serge and me in range. I know guns. There are some advantages to being born into a family of cops.

"Marc, it's me, Kelly," I said. "Drop the gun. You don't want to kill anybody."

"Stay away," shouted Serge. "He'll kill you."

"Nobody's going to get killed," I said, wishing that Serge would just shut up and praying that Ken would hurry.

Marc skated toward me. I tried to back away. I had forgotten when I stepped out onto the ice how much faster a person can move on skates. That was dumb. With Marc on skates and me in street shoes, Marc could easily keep me within range of his gun, no matter what its caliber.

"Kelly, you shouldn't have interfered," said Marc sadly. "I don't want to hurt you."

"Then don't," I said. Marc skated in circles in front of me.

"You're a good skater," I said stupidly. As last words, they weren't going to go down in history.

"Do you hear that, Serge?" shouted Marc to his captive judge. "She thinks I'm good."

"Very good," I shouted.

"Good enough to make the Olympic team," bragged Marc. I hoped he wouldn't shoot while he was bragging.

Marc did a double axle. I hoped he would fall, but he didn't. At least he was out of breath.

"I could have made it if you hadn't told her I was too unstable," Marc gasped. "She said so, too. She would never have dropped me if you hadn't told her to. . . . You . . ."

"I never told her to drop you," said Serge. "That

was her decision. She's always been capricious. Look how she treated Ken."

Marc skated away from me toward Serge.

I unhooked Baxter's leash. I figured that Baxter and I didn't both have to die. "Run, boy," I said.

Baxter refused to leave me to my fate. Instead of running back into the stands, he tried to take off after Marc. Maybe he was much more of a watchdog than I'd ever known. He slid on the ice.

Out of the corner of his eye, Marc saw Baxter trying to run toward him. Marc raised his gun.

"Drop dead!" I shouted, falling to the ice on my stomach.

A shot rang out.

Baxter was lying completely still on the ice.

"You killed him!" I shouted. Then I saw Baxter's side moving up and down. A shadow moved behind Serge. A skater flew out onto the ice. Marc turned his gun on him.

"Alive!" I yelled to Baxter. That was the command to stop playing dead, the only other command Baxter had ever totally learned. He jumped up and barked. Marc turned toward the sound and Ken tackled him on the ice, sending Marc sliding into the judges' stand.

Serge screamed.

I saw Marc's gun slither across the ice. I dove for it, grabbed it, and stood up. Suddenly, all the lights in the arena went on at once. "POLICE!" shouted a voice over the loudspeaker.

"Drop your guns!" I heard Mom yell from close by.

"Mom, I'm the only one with a gun!" I shouted.

I don't know who got to me first, Mom, Baxter, or Ken. I didn't faint, but my legs kind of went out from under me. I ended up flat on my rear end on the ice.

But it was Ken who carried me to the side of the rink and sat me down, and it was Ken who held my hand and wouldn't let go until long after we were all safe in Watson's office.

19 It's Not Over Until the Fat Lady Sings

"I always knew he was unstable," said Serge. We were still in Watson's office. Even after a couple of hours of freedom, Serge kept rubbing his arms, trying to get the circulation back.

"He was from Lake Placid, you know," said Serge. "I knew him there. He wanted so much to be a skater. It's funny, Ken, his background wasn't that different from yours. His family was poor. They were caretakers for some people with a summer home, one of those huge 'camps.' "

"There's one difference between us," said Ken. "I'm not insane."

"No . . . but it was really you, Carey, who sent him around the bend," said Serge.

"Me!" exclaimed Mrs. Clifton.

"You took him under your wing just like you did Ken. Then you dropped him, like a hot potato." Serge turned to Ken. "He didn't have your talent, or your perseverance. He cracked."

"His employment record was clean," said Mom.

"We knew he had worked at a rink in Lake Placid."

"He knew everything there was to know about skating," said Serge. "Except how to deal with the pressures of being near the top. I never knew if he would have made it anyhow. Sometimes I thought Mrs. Clifton did him a favor by dropping him."

"I told you I wasn't to blame," said Mrs. Clifton. But her voice was subdued.

"But why did he attack Andre?" I asked. "Why not Ken? Ken was the one who replaced him as Mrs. Clifton's protégé."

"He did attack Ken first," said Serge. "But then he ran into Mrs. Clifton and she told him that Ken was more trouble than he was worth."

"How did you know that?" demanded Mrs. Clifton.

"Marc had plenty of time to talk to me all morning. He kept me tied up in that room with the basketball court."

"I fell on the rope that Marc had used," I said.

"Well, I did recognize him," said Mrs. Clifton. "Even with the beard. I was surprised to see Marc, and I thought I'd make him feel better by telling him that he wasn't the only skater who had ever been dropped. I told him I was no longer going to support Ken."

"That gave him the idea that he would have a chance again," said Serge.

160

"But I told him that I was going to sponsor Andre if Andre would agree to it," said Mrs. Clifton.

"Not in a million years," said Andre.

"But Marc didn't know that," said Serge. "That's why he attacked Andre. He had a crazy idea that if he could talk me into letting him skate tonight, his whole life would be different. Mrs. Clifton made Marc feel that he had a second chance."

"I recognized him down at the rink before the exhibition," said Mrs. Clifton. "But I never thought he was behind all these incidents."

"If you had told us what you knew, we could have stopped Marc right away," said Mom angrily.

Mrs. Clifton fluttered her hands in front of her face. "I just don't think like a detective."

"You just don't think," I mumbled. Mom heard me. She put her arms around me. I knew how happy she was that I was safe.

"When I got Mrs. Clifton's letter about Ken," said Serge, "it reminded me of how she treated Marc. I must have scribbled my old code word for him without thinking. Then this morning when I was at the rink early to watch Andre's patch, Marc attacked me. He insisted I let him skate instead of Andre. I refused. I didn't even know that Andre had been attacked until he came back for me later."

"Ben-Gay?" I said.

"What?" exclaimed Andre.

"Ben-Gay . . . that's why you thought it was Ken when you were attacked. Marc always smells of Ben-Gay. When Ken was in our bathroom, I noticed it smelled of it, too. And in his dressing room, he put on an ointment."

"It's not exactly Ben-Gay, but it smells like it," said Ken. "I always use it before and after I skate. It keeps my muscles warm."

"I knew it smelled familiar," said Andre.

"What a nightmare for both of you," Mrs. Clifton said to Serge and Andre, conveniently ignoring Ken and me.

"I would be dead," said Serge, "if it hadn't been for Kelly's courage, and Ken's."

"Ken, perhaps I was too hasty . . ." stammered Mrs. Clifton.

Ken cut her off. "Forget it," he snapped. "Mrs. Clifton, you can take your money and . . ."

"Ken," cautioned Serge.

"I'd give up skating before I'd take a penny from her."

Mom's phone broke the awkward silence. She spoke into it a minute. "David needs me. He's finished interrogating Marc, and they're going to book him. He's being taken to Bellevue for some tests. You'll excuse me."

"I need to practice," said Ken. "I still have a performance tonight."

Serge started to stand up. His face was white.

"I'll go with you," he said. "Mrs. Clifton, you'll never sponsor another skater of mine."

Andre stood up, too. "In fact," he said to Ken, "I'll do some fund raising for you."

"That won't be necessary," said Watson. "I'll be very pleased to pay for the rest of Ken's training."

Ken rolled his eyes. I laughed. I guess he realized that Watson would not be the easiest patron in the world, either.

I got up to go with them. "No," said Ken. "I need to practice without any more distractions."

Suddenly I was a distraction. Ken must have seen the hurt on my face. "I'm sorry, Kelly. But tonight I've got to make it good."

Serge put his arm around me. "You are not going to be left out in the cold," he said. "Don't worry. Tonight, Ken will skate beautifully." He winked at me. "And it will not be the last time he skates against Andre. It's not over till the young lady sings, I promise you."

I didn't tell him that it was "until the fat lady sings."

Mrs. Clifton turned to me. "I never meant to encourage Marc," she said. "It was such a surprise to see him. I just told him that Ken was a handful, too. I thought it would make him feel good. How could I know it would send him around the bend? And as for dropping Ken . . . well, he *is* a difficult person."

163

I stood up. "Excuse me, Mrs. Clifton," I said. "I think I hear the fat lady singing."

"What?" she asked.

I smiled at her. "It's over, Mrs. Clifton. Nobody wants your money. It costs too much."

"You, young lady, are very insulting."

"And so are you, ma'am," I said.

Mrs. Clifton gathered up her furs. "Well," she said, "I can see that I am not wanted."

"Go sponsor a professional wrestler," I said. "They'll appreciate your honesty." Then I was sorry I had said that. Even Hulk Hogan didn't deserve Mrs. Clifton.

20 You Are to Die For

The spotlight was on Andre. He moved with the fluid grace that was his alone. The small patch on the back of his head was covered with makeup.

Ken stood in the runway, practicing his steps in his skateguards. He was totally concentrated.

Andre finished his routine to thunderous applause. He skated over to Serge, his breath coming in rasps.

Ken took off his skateguards. He handed them to me, and then he skated out to do his warm-ups while the judges rated Andre's performance.

Andre's scores were high. All 9.8s and 9.9s. There was little room for Ken to beat him.

The music for Ken's routine filled the arena. Andre stood beside me, leaning his arms against the barricade as he watched Ken skate. Andre's head nodded every time Ken completed a move.

When it came time for Ken's quadruple, Andre sucked in his breath.

Ken flew around the perimeter of the rink, skating backward faster and faster. His body was almost parallel to the ice and it looked as if he was bound to fall. When the curve was at the tightest, Ken launched the edge of his skate into orbit, his body a tight spiral, a blur. He turned, once, twice, three times, his body losing momentum. You could see his muscles straining as he pulled himself around a fourth time.

He landed it! A huge grin spread across his face. Only then did I realize I had been holding my breath, too.

Andre shook my hand. "He nailed it," he whispered. "He nailed it."

Ken went into his final spin. He threw his fist into the air triumphantly.

Then he stood still while he waited for the judges' scores. The roar of the crowd told it all—a solid row of 9.9s. He had beaten Andre. It might be just an exhibition, but for that one night, Ken was a champion.

Ken skated slowly around the rink, savoring his victory, like a baseball player who had just hit a towering grand slam. Dozens of girls came down from the stands to throw roses at his feet. He picked them up and gathered them in his arms, until his arms were so full that he could carry no more.

He finally skated to the side where we were standing. Andre was the first one to congratulate

Ken. Then he turned to Serge. "It's time for me to start practicing the quad."

Sweat poured off Ken's face.

Ken looked back up at the scoreboard at the row of 9.9s. He looked down at me. He handed me the roses in his arms. "Here," Ken said. "These are for you. You are to die for."

And then he kissed me, sweat and all.